MY LIFE V
YOUR LIFE

To Katie —

my good wish —

MY LIFE WITH SPIRIT, YOUR LIFE WITH SPIRIT

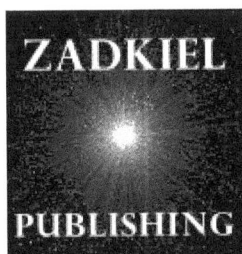

ZADKIEL

PUBLISHING

To walk the spiritual path is to continually step out
into the unknown.
Wallace Huey

Introduction

"You will know the truth, and the truth will set you free" (John 8:32 The Holy Bible).

Words that have resonated with me since I was a child, finding a personal faith in Jesus Christ that no one wanted to know about, and those who I did tell often derided me. Twenty years after finding that faith I sat in a cold church one autumn night preparing to lead worship when, the Spirit within me took me to the top of God's mountain, where a voice so real it could have been standing right next to me said, "this is your last time here. No more will you come to my mountain until you have discovered the truth and journeyed further along your life's path. Only then will you be free to come here again."

Sure enough, a week later I had left the church, my life seemingly falling to pieces.

Step forward another twenty years and a wonderful person came into my life. How that happened had to be planned by the angels for she lived on the Isle of Wight and I lived just outside London. Yet we met, and I knew instantly I had found my guide. More than that, as you will find later in this book, I sensed we had had a connection that went way back in time. We have been in touch almost every day since and though I know Dorothy thinks I am there for her, actually I KNOW she is there for me. Spirit works that way sometimes. She has been instrumental in my personal journey of finding the truth, gently leading me over the past few years in my own spiritual journey, and now I know I am free to go back up that mountain and discover the next stage of my journey. In many ways, after all these years, my journey is still just beginning.

I am thrilled and excited to be able to now publish Dorothy's autobiography. I urge you to read it and to use it to continue your own journey in life. I am sure you will find the same inspiration I have found and that you too will discover your journey will be uplifting, and fulfilling and my fervent hope and prayer is that your journey will bring you the kind of deep, inner peace, that only a true angel can bring you.

Stuart Holland, November 2017

MY LIFE WITH SPIRIT

(I have so much to share with you!)

The Journey Begins

This is a skeleton outline of a journey through a life that has truly been 'full of surprises', a prediction given during a reading I had fifty-seven years ago by a respected medium. I went with apprehension and excitement, holding on to the words my mother said, 'ask for a reading, nothing else' and still remember the sense of awe which swept over me as I sat with her. She took my ring and began to talk to me. Love life, beware of jumping out of the fire into the frying pan' – she was right about that. There was more which the years have erased. Then she said, 'I wish I could show you your life as I see it, full of surprises.' She was right about that, too. I remember the girls walking up her path as I left, two teens asking, 'can we have our fortunes told?' They were sent away with the sharp words 'I don't tell fortunes!' So, there was the reason for my mother's instructions. When I finally go home I will look for her and give her my heartfelt thanks. Her influence has persisted through my working life as a medium, her quiet way, her quiet voice, her sense of conviction in all she said and did, her surety of the words being right. Just as I know I am.

That's the main thing I recall and the one thing I am aware of; I know when I'm right. It's more than a 'knowing', it's going cold because spirit move in and make me go cold. A physical reaction to a non-physical happening, a physical reaction to a psychic happening, in effect. It happens when you're open to spirit 24-7 as I am, much to the dismay, sometimes disgust, sometimes anger of some mediums. They worry about my security, my sanity, my life. Why? I have rings of psychic defence, I have half a ton of love around me at any given moment and the spirits I love walk with me at all times.

Those mediums don't know what they're missing...

What is the most important part of me, the medium or the writer? My past lives reveal I was either a wise woman or scribe or writer of some kind or a combination of the two.

A priestess in Ancient Britain.
A wise woman in Alfred's time.
One of Henry's queens.
Scribe to Charles I.

Many lives, many experiences. In this life I've studied herbs and trained as a spiritual healer. In this life I have written many, many articles, stories and books. In this life I finally said, 'I want to be a medium.' (More accurately, I said, during the service in the first spiritualist church I attended, 'I want to do that.')

This life is where the two sides of me became one, the writer and healer became a channel for spirit authors, translating their words into modern English so people can read it, understand it and appreciate the nonsense historians have written about them over the years. Writing their life story helps them heal. This life is the last one I will live on this side of the divide: I have work to do when I go home. It's good to know I've almost achieved everything spirit wanted me to do.

Let's not forget I was not unwilling: everything I've done was agreed to before birth. This isn't something every spiritually minded person believes but I do and so do many others. It's the only thing which makes sense of why we experience such things as illness, accident, deep lasting sorrow, poverty, or conversely, good health, wealth, love and comfort. We need to be sure that the lessons we learn are the ones which will help us on our onward progression as spirits.

There is a way to go before then. I experienced much before I opened myself to spirit. This is a good point to say I'd already opened myself to Christ. I carry the faith of a Christian into the work of being a medium. I don't consider myself a Christian Spiritualist as such, but He is part of my spiritual life.

My 74 years sit easy on me tonight; this book is beginning to flow. It has been a while since I wrote anything, I now realise the time had to be right. Everything spirit does is all mapped out, but you can only see it when you look back. The paranormal site I visited every day closed down. The historical organisation where I helped out closed down. The writing site, the centre of my writing life, closed down. What was left was time to write this book.

Spirit always get their own way. Be sure of that!

***

I arrived in this physical life in 1943, a war baby. It would be boring for you if I was to relate the family life at the time, but I need to slide a comment in here which was to follow me for many years, my mother saying, 'I think I brought the wrong baby home from hospital.' Because I am so unlike all the rest. Not physically, I am a copy of one of my cousins, we could be interchangeable, but mentally and, I later discovered, spiritually. The spirit side of my current life can be seen in hindsight, but none of us realised it at the time. I was just 'odd.'

Many children have 'invisible friends' (spirit children) to play with. I had a friend also called Dorothy. We spent hours together, discovering the world in a garden full of flowers, trees and vegetables, always something to explore, things to work out. Later I dropped her, as it were, and concentrated on being many things, a code breaker, copying the odd graffiti on brick walls and signposts, looking for the connections, looking for signs. It is only now, looking back down the tunnel of years, do I realise that I was then looking for signs, indicators, directions for my life which seemed aimless and pointless. I went to school, I wrote stories that had the teachers asking for more, I ignored the subjects I didn't like (such as art, I wrote poems on the back of the paper instead). I discovered books and the skills an author can bring by using words to make a character live. I read everything I could find, from my father's Western collection to the children's encyclopaedias which raised more questions than they answered.

I remember sitting with my mother's special china cup. It had little squares inside with tiny pictures in them. I finally discovered that you drank the tea, then swilled the remainder around in the cup, tipped it upside down in a saucer and looked to see where the leaves were. (This was before the magical tea bag was invented, of course.) That was your fortune.

My mother had an often-quoted statement; 'I brought the wrong baby home from hospital'. When she found a true story in a magazine of a woman who did really take home the wrong baby, the child's blood group didn't match either parent, this added to her belief I was 'wrong'. I felt wrong. I felt out of place.

My sister arrived when I was five years old. I don't remember my mother going to hospital for the birth, so if this was a home confinement, she couldn't say she had brought the wrong baby home for a second time. My sister was 'all right.'

I started Sunday School at the age of seven. I don't remember how long it was before I took Christ as my personal Saviour after an evangelical preacher came to talk to us, but I remember doing it. I discovered two Sundays later I was the only person who had. All the others looked so blank it was almost laughable. I was young, yes, but the faces gave it away. No one else had taken the message to heart. The Sunday School teacher asked why I hadn't said anything at the time, that 'Uncle Fred' would have been pleased to know. I wondered why I hadn't said anything. From this distance of time I think it was a private thing between Jesus and me, not something to tell to anyone else, even if that other person had been the one to open my heart and mind. I keep a lot to myself even now; it's not a bad habit to cultivate.

Was this me looking for something outside my day to day life? My lovely Nan gave me a bible, which I still have. Her inscription is dated 1955. I used to look at the colour illustrations, put the little biblical texts we got from Sunday School teachers in the appropriate pages, everything except try and read it and make sense of it all. It was too early in my development, I now know, and too isolated from the way my family thought, too. No one said grace; no one went to church outside of weddings, christenings and the inevitable funerals. Religion, as I heard about it in Sunday School, didn't match what my family did. I had no way of knowing many were like that.

My family was large, loads of aunts, uncles and cousins, most of whom gathered at Nan's house every weekend. How much I picked up there cannot be really separated from the memories of the gatherings, but I became aware that at least one neighbour 'read the tea leaves' which confused me and that another aunt was asking 'Lily' to leave her alone. How I knew Lily was in the spirit world is another mystery of that time. It was many years before I discovered who she was, one of Nan's children who didn't survive.

It was at one of these gatherings an uncle gave me two magazines he thought I might like: *Fantasy and Science Fiction* and *Astounding*. Would I like them! I devoured them, especially Ray Bradbury's story in F&SF. Through them I discovered fandom, that wonderful world of like-minded people who wrote endless letters, went to conventions, produced their own fanzines and seemed to like what I was writing at the time.

I created my own fanzine, only one issue, which I called Trial. Double meaning, would it work/I was a junior in a solicitor's office. Writing was emerging as something I not only wanted to do, but had to do. The magazine wasn't the answer, but it was worth the effort just to get feedback.

I was working in the City of London, a place of shades and shady places, intricate ancient paths leading into courtyards or to the main streets of the main place, the financial centre of England. There were booksellers in virtually every street I walked; I bought Ray Bradbury's books to read on the train to and from work.

I also bought Lobsang Rampa's 'The Third Eye' (without knowing why) and couldn't understand it. That was immaterial; the fact remained there was an emptiness at times, a longing at other times, a need for information without knowing what the information was I needed and that was a start. I tried to read Betty Shine's books, but they didn't make sense, my lack of knowledge of the spirit world, of mediums, tarot readers and everyone else, rendered them useless to me.

Again, at this distance of time, I can't remember what prompted me to ask where I could get a reading. Maybe a magazine article or someone at work? Either seems logical. Whatever the reason, I was directed to Mrs Palmer, an elderly lady who held an item belonging to the sitter to make her connection. I don't think she needed it, she just did it. That was when she told me my life was full of surprises.

I heard a story later which may or may not be true, but it fits the lady I met. The story is that a young man went to see her, she took his ring, held it, then handed it back and said, 'sorry, here's your money back, there's no one there.' The young man was killed the next day on his motorbike. If this is true, it's an object lesson for any medium on how to handle bad news.

I found out recently that the first real help and advice the international medium Stephen O'Brien had was from a Mrs Palmer. This is not the same person, mine was in Essex, his was in Wales, but what a nice coincidence.

For the sake of continuity, of mentioning his name, I want to slide in a little anecdote here as I can't remember exactly where it comes in my spiritual history. I'm sure you won't mind.

We had a meeting at which the medium told me I was full of questions and that I would find all my answers on page 132 of a particular book by Stephen O'Brien. As it happened... some of us in the meeting had tickets to see Stephen O'Brien who was giving a demonstration here on the island. I had three weeks to wait to get my answers...

On the night I went over to his sales stall with great anticipation, bought the book and hurried back to my seat where friends were waiting. I flipped through the pages – it was one of those books where the new chapter started on a new page, regardless of where the previous chapter finished. Page 132 was blank. We collapsed with laughter, it was so obvious, find your own answers. I do now, all the time. I still can't get over how precise that message was, right down to the page number.

By the way, it was a brilliant demonstration by Stephen O'Brien, names, house numbers, road names, personal information and moving messages. He's one fine medium.

I read more than I wrote at that time, not a bad thing. I listened to a lot of radio drama, serials in particular, which meant I absorbed the concept of cliff hangers. The short stories were a challenge, one I tried to live up to, but there was a lot of writing to do before I got it right.

I was married in church, aged nineteen. It meant a lot. My new husband was a tall suave good-looking soldier, wearing dress uniform, serving with the City of London Fusiliers.

When he was demobbed I thought life was going to be wonderful. Instead it crashed, eighteen months exactly from the date we were married, casting me out into a cold world where others were preparing to be married and I was single again. (It was too much to ask a twenty-one-year-old to wait ten years for a registered paedophile to be released from prison. I was advised to divorce him.)

Through this I rediscovered my Christian faith, was confirmed into the Church of England and found a refuge in a cold world. Everything was related to God, all the signs I know now were spirit

I allocated to God. It comforted me, and I think that was right for me then.

As a family we emigrated to Spain and then came what was really the first amazing 'happening', which I gave back to God. I was 'governess' to the Deputy Mayor of Bilbao's three youngest children. (My task was to teach them English.) I went to work by train. One day I realised I only had enough money for a one-way ticket. It was going to be a long walk back home. I was early, so I slipped into a chapel, knelt down and asked for help. When I opened my eyes, every statue in the chapel wore a halo of gold light. I went to work with a lighter heart.

The Deputy Mayor's wife met me in the playroom. 'Here you are,' she said, handing me my wages for the month. 'I thought you'd like this a week early.'

Is it that simple? Yes, it is. It's called Trust.

***

Life moves on, brings us new people, new experiences. My days were filled with commuting to the City of London, trying out all the branches of law, including a job as a secretary to two young solicitors starting their own practice in Temple, the hallowed grounds of the legal world. All of this featured in my writing in later years, that was when I realised how much I'd absorbed.

In this world, this strange formal world of the legal profession came another big happening, one I didn't recognise then but now see it for what it was;

an explosion of light in my mind which I immediately shut down. It was fearful, it was scary; it was not capable of being explained. From this distance of time I wonder why and how the need to learn more about being psychic and/or mediumistic had managed to slip away, but it had.

I was working as a legal clerk. I took a client to Temple for a conference with Counsel. The Chambers as a whole seemed interested in me, once again, I was different, they kept saying. The clerk asked where I'd learned to prepare the papers for the barristers, as he hadn't seen anything like it for years. I learned from the very old solicitor in my first job, one who demanded precision and got it. The instructions started 'put the brass split pin one inch in from the corner. Any less and the sheets will tear off in court. Any more and Counsel would not be able to turn the pages properly.' That kind of training you don't forget.

The client left, the barrister and I drank tea. I asked about another member of chambers who had fallen awkwardly and broken his elbow. It had set in such a way he couldn't wear a normal coat. He was refusing surgery and had taken to wearing a cloak instead of a coat. Quite how this next part came about I don't know, but I began saying this barrister was doing it for effect, he could easily be cured but that would take away the 'difference'. He liked being eccentric, different. I then described his wife (I had never met any of their wives) and could see by the shocked look I was right. I went on to describe other barristers' wives but before I could begin on the wife of the barrister I sat with, he said it was enough... now I realise I had shaken him considerably and he didn't really want to know any more. It was so clear to me: all their wives, all their foibles, all their ambitions were there to be read in the fraught atmosphere of Chambers.

I now know I simply 'read' the atmosphere and translated it into words. Back then it was nothing more than a mysterious event.

***

I found a new love and made a commitment to marriage, believing this time it would be all right. The biological clock was ticking; I needed the child my new husband said he wanted, needed it in good time before I couldn't produce anything.

I was by then working in a solicitors' office directly opposite St Bride's in Fleet Street. The church rang the bell for lunch time communion and once a week I would race down three flights of stairs, cross the road – risking life and limb to do it – and enter the coolness and tranquillity of the church. There was a statue of the Mother by the door and it was there my prayers were directed, please let me be like you, let me bear a child. I knew, without anyone ever confirming it, that I had become pregnant eighteen months earlier but the doctor I saw took advantage of my need to know to do an unnecessary internal examination. I bled immediately afterwards. This isn't gratuitous gore by the way; it features later in my spirit life story. I'm setting things out as they happened.

The prayers were heard. I became pregnant at the age of thirty. We are talking over forty years ago; the hospital treated me like some kind of freak. Older mothers weren't so widely known then.

Our child arrived, the blonde, blue eyed girl my husband wanted.

Somewhere around this time was a Happening, as I began to think of them, but quite what I was doing in that small church at that time I don't recall. Perhaps visiting for a quiet prayer session? Being a stay-at-home mother wasn't much fun after working in the City for close on fifteen years, with churches everywhere for me to find solace from the frantic world. (A side comment: that solace has been taken away from so many people. Churches are locked against the vandalism responsible for wrecking so many, or they have been made redundant. One of my chosen charities is the Churches Conservation Trust.)

Enough of trying to remember, the fact is I had been reading Catherine Marshall's books on her husband Peter Marshall, Chaplain to the Senate, a man who walked closely with Jesus. He had a visual style of writing which impressed me. I'm saying this as I used to blame this happening on my over active imagination from reading his books. In one he spoke of 'hearing the Lord's robes move as he walked.'

This quiet day, possibly a communion service, the feeling is coming closer that it was; I sat in a pew - alone. I heard robes swishing, I heard the creak of the floorboards, I felt the pew bend slightly under the weight of someone and definitely felt the arm which went around my shoulders. The rush of love that swept through me is beyond my ability to describe.

I risked opening my eyes. There was no one there. There was no one my side of the church at all.

***

The writing was the important thing at that time. I had a portable typewriter, I had a table; I worked. All that I had learned from many rejections and acceptances came back, so I was not really surprised when a fanfic story based on the SF series Blake's Seven was instantly accepted by the fanzine and I was asked for more.

Again, I will not bore you with the long drawn out apprenticeship that is writing, but it progressed very fast. By then our daughter was growing up, going to school, coming home with drawings and thoughts which I translated into humorous plays and books for schools. I had progressed from a table to a desk in an alcove to a custom-built room of my own, to us moving to a three-bedroom house so I could have the third bedroom to write.

In the middle of all this, I had an overwhelming desire to dissect the four Gospels and, using them as my basis, wrote out the life of Jesus. No teachings or preachings, just his life. I think I was about ¾ of the way through when Jehovah's Witnesses called. I almost leapt on them and bombarded them with this work, how magical it was, how it made Jesus come alive… they said very little, just left as soon as they could. The book was called Living In The Shadow Of The Cross, taken from a quote made by a medieval monk, who said something like 'life is but a shadow cast by the Cross, so we are all living in the shadow of the cross.'

I finished the book but – usual mixed reactions, lay people loved it, clergy hated it. So it was filed and for a time, forgotten.

If there were signs during that time, I wasn't aware of them. I should have been, the way the pieces fell into place. For example, I wrote a long poem for my daughter about Humpty Dumpty. My mother read it, showed it to a friend who said, 'I can see that being acted out in schools.' I turned it into a play and sent it to the first educational publisher I discovered in the writers' handbook – and they accepted it. Distance learning creative writing tutoring work, all there, falling into my lap. Articles, short stories, photographs, all accepted. Sign after sign I managed to miss by simply turning off the part of me which once searched news of or from the other side.

I went to Holy Communion once a month and served the Flower Guilds at two churches for a good many years. It was solace for a mind much troubled by many things, including the 'missing' element which I sought, without knowing it, for so long.

Coming Out Of The Darkness

Everything changes, everything dies/ends. This is a tough one to accept but it's true. That and the other old adage, there is nothing so permanent as change, should help us accept major happenings in our lives, but we are never truly prepared. The ending of my twenty-three-year marriage is one example. I'd thought being cast out in the cold, unwelcoming world after my first breakup was bad, this was much worse. I had, over the years, developed the habit of relying on someone other than me. To be confronted with the need to change my life completely was terrifying.

Or seemed to be when it happened. The strength came from somewhere; I went to bed inconsolable; I woke with a surge of determination. I went straight to the Estate Agents and put the house on the market, without waiting for any discussion on finances.

I need to backtrack just a little here, to show how the hand of spirit was so clearly in all of this. I had taken a copy-editing course; I had obtained distance editing work from a small company on the Isle of Wight. We had travelled there to meet the directors in March of that year; my husband said he wanted to leave in June. I phoned the director I was most friendly with, the wonderful Terry Wakelin, who told me to get the next ferry over and go house hunting. He would guarantee me a job.

We visited the island; we put notes through Estate Agents' doors asking for details of three-bedroom houses or flats. Within a week my daughter and I were viewing the flat we now live in, twenty-three years on.

We moved in November of that year, arriving on the Friday and me starting work on the Monday. It all seemed like a dream and yet this was reality. It had all fallen into place. The flat needed endless repairs, the money was there to do it as my husband didn't claim any of the proceeds of the sale. The flat still needs repairs, a lot of it, but it has given us shelter and sanctuary for all these years. I hope I don't have to move for some time, but I am aware of increasing/developing arthritis.

During my work at the publishers, I learned to use Pagemaker, a programme that turns a manuscript into a booklet or book. I had no idea at first how this would be of such benefit to me, but I knew all learning was good, so I found out everything the programme could do. Today IT people laugh at Pagemaker and want me to change to In Design, the answer is -forget it, I know Pagemaker and I won't need it forever, anyway. The last issue is to be Winter 2023. The skeleton outline is already in place.

The first year was all work, getting the flat the way we wanted it, no small feat as it's actually three storeys in all. I found my way around the island; I got on well at work.

I also realised I was becoming psychic. Strange that, after so many years, I should realise what was happening, although I had it backwards. I wasn't

25

becoming psychic; I was opening up to being psychic. I was sensing people, knowing when they were coming, whether they were all right, that kind of thing.

It was at this point spirit took a hand and shook everything up.

Before I go into that, let me say now that the flat we found is 'haunted' or, if you like, has spirits still living in it and using it.

The first thing I became aware of was the three times a week gathering of men with their dogs. They stand around in the lounge, a huge room 21' in length, plenty of room for them all. They talk, they drink, they gamble.

I can't hear anything they're saying, they don't seem to be aware I'm there and they take no notice whatsoever of my spirit companions. It is as if they're trapped or enclosed in their own time capsule, they do the same things, the pattern is always the same. So… discounting the fact I can't see them, I think they're ghosts, a fragment of history trapped in a time loop.

The other spirits are more obvious. I have had someone come into my bedroom and take a book from a shelf I don't have. The sound of the other books falling over is quite distinctive; whoever took the book just let the others fall.

I've had someone come into my bedroom and open the flap of a bureau I don't have. I speak to these people, I get no response or recognition they've heard me. I don't think they're ghosts, the activity hasn't been repeated.

I've laid awake listening to a conversation going on outside my bedroom door between a man and a woman. I can't understand a word being said, it's as if it's muffled by something, but they're emphatic about the subject under discussion.

I've heard footsteps coming up the stairs to the bedrooms.

My daughter smelled cigarette smoke in our lounge a good thirty minutes before I did, and she swears she isn't psychic…

She's smelled cigar smoke in my office.

I'm aware if I come downstairs to the bathroom in the night it's a good idea to put a robe on as the spirit I believe is Mr Carlton Bull emerges from what is now my office/study and stands there, watching.

Confirmation of this: We know from the deeds that Mr Carlton Bull owned the property fairly recently, in property terms, that is, and traded as a high-class jeweller. Brian Rice, my friend, used to work for the ironmongers almost directly opposite the property, which in those days had stairs going from the middle of the downstairs shop floor up to the store rooms/living accommodation above. We live there in the part which has been sealed off from downstairs. Brian used to carry the bottles of gas from the ironmongers across the road and up the stairs into Mr Carlton Bull's flat. He confirmed Mr Bull smoked thin cigars and also mentioned, as a side comment, that he had an eye for the ladies…

Now my home is 'haunted' by those who work with me. I know them all and trust them all. The other activity doesn't bother me. It's been quite a few years since anyone has come into my bedroom to get something so that phase seems to have passed, they now realise (perhaps) they needed to move on. Mr Carlton Bull is still around, I walk down the stairs at night into the coldness only spirit radiate but I intend to continue to disappoint him with any display of flesh. Eventually he too will get tired and move on.

So, where was I? Oh yes, Spirit's 'interference' in my progression.

My flat is two doors away from an arcade which dates back to Queen Victoria. I pushed, literally, into visiting, going into a small room and asking a tarot reader I had never seen before to give me a reading. I had never seen a pack of tarot cards before, either. Everything felt strange, everything felt right. She shuffled the pack, laid out the spread, turned over the first card and said, 'you're very spiritual, do you sit circle?'

I had no idea what she meant. I didn't want to appear to be totally stupid, so I fluffed and muttered my way through the reading. I don't remember any more, that was what registered, that was what would not leave my mind. I made enquiries and found out there was a spiritualist church right there in town.

The President was a stickler for doing things properly. I think I called her or wrote to ask about sitting circle. She asked me to visit her in her office at the church before the service started, to make sure it was not just imagination. 'My dear, I have seen that so often with young girls.' I visited, as she asked. I sat perfectly still for about a minute, then she said, 'go on into the church.' I had passed her test anyway.

It was the first time I had been in a spiritualist church, so I had no idea what to expect. It looked more church-like than I had anticipated; a portrait of Jesus over the platform, church type sliding boards for the numbers of the hymns, everything was (almost) the same as the churches I was well used to. The difference came with the address (sermon) followed by messages.

The medium was Charles Samway, who spoke for a while and then began giving messages. Two things happened: one was the lady next to me thought he was talking to her and when she realised he wasn't, her wave of disappointment flooded over me. I had never experienced that, it was almost complete empathy. The other thing was, after Mr Samway gave me a short message, I sent out a thought *'I want to do that'*. The eyes were open at last; I knew what I wanted to do. I saw how people gained comfort from the messages; I wanted to bring that comfort.

As with a conventional church, it's the custom for the medium and whoever is chairing the service to leave the platform before the congregation moves. Mr Samway walked up the aisle, stopped by my side and simply stared at me. I could feel power and strength, but had no idea what message he was trying silently to give me. I was aware the President was getting edgy and moved him on.

That was his last platform appearance. A short time later I heard of his passing.

I was invited to sit in the church development circle and so began my training in a small select group, meditating to the sound of Pan pipes. (I have to confess I've hated them ever since.) I learned about protection, creating a kind of shield against anything or anyone that would like to take advantage of someone wide open to the spirit world during meditation. There is more on this in the sections where I've included all the information you should need for your onward journey.

On one 'momentous' occasion I was invited to sit in the President's home circle to experience table tilting, among other things. I went because I was keen to experience all aspects of spirit work, if I could.

I soon realised everyone was having a good time, the table was rocking and moving and there were lights going over everyone's hands. Except mine. I hated the whole experience and was very pleased when I could escape. The President told everyone how the little hall table would 'walk' down the hall at night to meet her when she came in. I didn't say anything; I didn't feel it warranted a comment. I couldn't prove it happened, so how could I applaud it happening? I still don't know precisely why it bothered me so much, perhaps there's an element of not wanting spirit to waste their energy on something that's all show. They have far more important work to do than that.

Like all good things, if I can say the slightly prickly time I spent visiting Ryde church was good, it had to come to an end. I read Psychic News every week, in particular the letters section. I had it in mind to write a general observation which, of course, was taken as a personal insult.

I said – in essence – the mediums asked to take a service are not putting on a performance. Therefore, it's wrong for the members of the congregation to get their tea and then stand around making comments such as 'not very good, was she?' if every message wasn't taken in its entirety.

I didn't see the paper the day it was printed, but I found out soon enough they had included it when the President all but threw a copy at me before circle started. Her anger was almost physical. She also handed me a letter. The contents made me want to laugh out loud but it would have added unwarranted fuel to the flames. It was from a Church Secretary on the mainland saying he agreed with every word. Not one person in the circle wanted to read it. I knew only too well every one of them knew I was right, they had been guilty of it themselves, but hated to be shown up.

In this poisonous atmosphere we had a meditation. When we came back to 'real life', one of the sitters said, 'what I got was words, how they can be used to hurt or insult.' So she hadn't gone anywhere during the meditation, she'd sat and fumed. Her loss of the best part of half an hour... along with any friendship I felt for her. It never was right between us after that.

Two weeks later the President took the service and indulged in her usual habit of wandering down the aisle – something the SNU frowns on, protocol says you do not leave the platform during a service – telling people about their 'lights'. She stopped by my side and, with the most overwhelming lack of enthusiasm, said she could see her lights going to me. I pretty much knew then I was on my way to being the medium I wanted to be.

It was then Brian Rice asked if I would like to join Ventnor church instead.

I agreed.

Going to Ventnor church was like coming out of the darkness. There were tensions, there is underlying tension whenever a group of people meet regularly, but the atmosphere was entirely different and, what's more, there were Fledgling Evenings.

These evenings were specifically for people who wanted to try out their clairvoyance without the formality of the Sunday service. The 'audience' was anyone who was kind enough to come and be a recipient of any messages that might be going. I remember being nervous, as anyone is speaking in public. I fastened my attention on a guy in the front row, someone I knew. I said I could see a young man standing on the pavement swinging a crash helmet. He said he wants to say hi to you. Could he take that?

He said 'that's my friend; he was killed in a motorcycle accident. He comes back every year at this time. I don't know why.' (I gathered later that it was the anniversary of the young man's accident). It was the confirmation I needed, which we all need when we work, someone to tell us we've got it right.

I used the Fledgling Evenings to work on clairvoyance and public speaking, which was useful, as before long I was chairing the Sunday services.

Another side-line, forgive me; I have to tell you things as I think of them. One of the things I did at Ventnor was take over the newsletter as no one else wanted to do it. I soon found there was more material than each newsletter could carry, so I began collecting up the poems, snippets, quotes and other items and got an idea (or was I pushed?) to make it into a magazine along the lines of the lovely Grace magazine then on public sale. I told Terry about this and said I wanted a good title for my new little magazine. He was halfway down the stairs one night at the office when he stopped and called up, 'Circle of Light. Just thought of it.'

The Circle of Light was produced, put on sale at the church and immediately ran into a problem. A visiting medium decided it wasn't 'right', it shouldn't be on sale and demanded it be removed. So I took it away from the church, their loss, it deprived them of additional income. I began advertising it in Psychic News and other places. Before long I had a substantial subscriber list for a forty-page spiritualist magazine which went to people in all parts of the UK and abroad. Even now, nineteen years on, I have four subscribers in the USA.

Simple fact: If that medium had not insisted it should not be on sale, countless people would not have read all the uplifting and educational spiritual items, poems and quotes I have used over the years. I know by the letters I receive how much it has meant to a great many subscribers. My mother had a piece of philosophy I've never forgotten: look for the good that comes out of the bad. The magazine fiasco could have been bad, for a while it was, but the good which came out of it is incalculable. One day that medium may find out, through this book or the last issue of the magazine, already set in my computer (Winter 2023) where I have spelled out this sorry tale, just what she did to accidentally promote my work to the world where it would have stayed in Ventnor. I realise now spirit had a hand in all of it.

Brian Rice invited me to sit in his home circle. The circle fluctuated between seven and ten people, really too many but it did build a lot of energy. They were powerful occasions. There were trance communications every week; we had phenomena like tapes not working so the sessions couldn't be recorded. One tape had piano music on it when the CD was of orchestral music.

One evening a crazy/funny spirit who said he was Daniel came through Brian in his trance state and began to talk to us. The circle sitters were, on the whole, used to the 'heavy' spirit guides coming, those who would give us philosophy (most of which went straight over my head.) They didn't know what to make of a spirit visitor who laughed and joked with us. I could feel the disapproval flowing from some of them. Daniel liked to talk to me because I would laugh with him. It really didn't go down well with the sitters, though. He told us he had been searching for fifty years for a circle to accept him, that they all said, 'thank you, friend, now move on.' The same thing might have happened in this circle too, but I was there. I have always been the 'different' one and Daniel was the same. We connected on many levels.

One night Daniel came in a different form, a quieter, subdued spirit who told us his last incarnation had been as a concentration camp victim. He talked of being in the camp with Odette Churchill and was overcome with emotion.

This in a way was counter-productive; those who disliked the funny Daniel were now shamefaced for that dislike and, being human, resented him even more. But he persisted and eventually won a few people round.

One of the mediums who served Ventnor church was Hazel Butterworth, a very talented lady. (She is no longer with us, a victim of Alzheimer's, I am sad to say.) At that time she was very closely connected with spirit. She lived in Lymington and came over on the ferry. I would be waiting for her to pick her up and took her to Ventnor. This particular Sunday we went to lunch before the service and I started to tell her about Daniel and the two sides of this lovely spirit. She stopped eating, stared at me and then said, 'oh, that's what happened.'

She explained that one night she was sending out thoughts to a friend named Daniel who was ill. A figure appeared at the end of her bed wearing what she thought was pyjamas. He said: 'I am Daniel.'

The 'pyjamas' were the concentration camp clothes. There was all the confirmation I needed that this was real.

Daniel came often to circle and then asked if I would write his life story. This was in the late 90s, I was producing a regular newsletter for the church and doing my writing but had not thought of writing a book for spirit. I said yes, for what else could I do? Daniel had already become a beloved friend by this time.

The book took 2 ½ years to write. It was traumatic and heart-breaking in every way, for Daniel's life before the camp was worse than life in the camp so it was difficult for him to talk to me about it. Sometimes he would disappear for several months; then come back with renewed strength to carry on; other times he would throw an entire paragraph at me just before I drifted off to sleep, as if he couldn't bear to say the words. When they were written down, I understood completely.

Hazel and I talked often on the phone about Daniel because of his tricks. The clown side came out when things were going well. There was one time she called and asked me to tell, not ask, Daniel to return her Coptic cross. His response was, 'when she says please.' The cross turned up three months later in the base of a vase in her wardrobe…

There was the time he came rushing to me to say, 'the beautiful lady' as he always referred to her (when he wasn't calling her Hazelnuts, that is) would be mad with him as he'd knocked the flowers over. I called her and she said she wasn't aware of anything being knocked over. An hour later she phoned back. The flowers alongside a photograph had been tipped over. Fortunately for her they were artificial, or there would have been water everywhere…

There was the time he hid my pendulum, which isn't used for divination but for finding things. It disappeared from a metal box and I discovered it, three weeks later, in a wooden box. I had to wait to find it; no other pendulum does the job as well as that one.

Always the jokes, always the fun. One night when we were settling down for circle, Daniel went round all the sitters – there were a lot at that time – commenting on each one. I couldn't tell anyone why I was giggling… I mean, comments like 'look at his trousers! And they call me a clown!' (The sitter had arrived wearing golfing trousers…)

Daniel the clown, Daniel the tragic German Jew. All true clowns have two sides. Daniel proved this but has at last found the peace his spirit sought for many years.

It's impossible to write this life story in a proper logical sequence. If I were to intersperse Daniel's story with other anecdotes I want to pass on, you would lose the sense of it. So let me just say when the book was finished and published by the small independent publisher where I worked, Daniel was at last eased in his mind and moved into the realms to the point when one medium said he was more light than spirit. I had a new 'clown'. One day as I drove to work, Daniel came to ask, 'are you happy with the clown I have given you, sister?' I told him I was.

Daniel has been in and out of my life ever since. I've been told he's in charge of my security. He's my beloved clown.

The 'clown' Daniel referred to is Antony Woodville, KG, Lord Scales of Newcelles and the Isle of Wight, 2nd Earl Rivers, my past life husband, my constant companion, my advisor, my everyday guide and my dearest love. There will be more about Antony later in the book, once I've worked through all the other many things I want/need to tell you! It's stopped being 'I want to write this' and is now 'you need to write this' with nudges and reminders in the middle of the night if I wake. I just cleared a pile of notes from the desk by my side, typed them into a 'don't forget' folder in the computer and still keep thinking of things…

Forgive the side-lines here and there, if I don't drop them in when I think of them, or where they connect with someone I'm writing about, they'll get missed.

I mentioned Hazel Butterworth.

Hazel was responsible for introducing me to my Mayan guide, Redwood. She casually mentioned during a service, 'by the way, there's a Mayan standing alongside you. He's your main guide.' It surprised me because at the time I'd fallen into the spiritualist trap of thinking all guides were Native Americans. It was foolish of me, my 'newbie' guide was a Mandarin, so I should have remembered they were all nationalities. Mayan is unusual, though, it raises a few eyebrows even now.

He took the name Redwood as his Mayan name is very complicated, as is mine. He told me I had been his senor concubine back when we were together, a time before the great ruined cities we see now. He said there were cities before them which also ended up as ruins, so we are talking countless thousands of years ago. Redwood was a priest-king. My task was to take care of his headdresses, all ceremonial, each with their special meaning. Over time I've ended up with five portraits of him by different psychic artists, which means I see him at

38

different stages of his physical life and even more important, with different headdresses which I recognise.

I commissioned four portraits of Redwood by different artists and then asked for one of Leslie Flint's Cockney guide Mickey, who came through regularly when we sat circle at Brian's. The portrait arrived and I found the artist had included another drawing; she said the person had pushed his way in. It was my fifth Redwood portrait.

I had one particularly vivid meditation where I saw him standing before the altar holding a severed head by its hair, blood running down the steps to the platforms below. It was shocking to me in this life but not in that, when it was a way of life.

An in-depth reading on Redwood by spirit artist Ann Davies revealed this lovely man has been with me through every single life I have lived. Sometimes he shared the material side of life with me, but mostly he was on the other side, guiding me from the Realms. Our love is amazing. Ann said in effect that every time I returned to the Realms and we were reunited, it was as if that life had been no more than a bad dream.

One thing he taught me, which has been of great benefit, is the Mayan way of divination. No archaeologist has discovered anything about this, because of the way it was done. There are no lasting artefacts.

He said the priests marked out a piece of ground using a stick to draw a rectangle, which they then divided into three parts by scoring two lines. The three sections represented Past, Present and Future. They had fifty stones, ordinary stones which had been selected for their shape, colour and size. Every one represented something, Love, Family, Life, Food, Health, you name it there was a stone for it. These were kept in a huge golden bowl. When the priests wanted to consult the gods in a physical fashion they threw the stones onto the marked out ground and then spent three days working out the message, which stones were next to which, touching/not touching, outside the lines, inside the lines, which section they had fallen into and how that affected their message.

It's extremely involved and extremely accurate. I found a large piece of material, sewed ribbon onto it to mark the sections, collected tumbled pebbles of different colours and types and naming them. The first reading I did when I'd conquered all of this took 1 ½ hours and was a truly spiritual experience.

Then my mother passed with cancer.

I was calm, I did the eulogy without a flutter; I drove back to the island and thought I could get on with life.

I wanted to do another reading. Nothing. The meanings of the stones had been wiped from my mind, all fifty of them. Grief is a strange thing; you never know how it's going to affect you. I ended up with a huge blank where the knowledge of the stones once roosted very comfortably.

I couldn't face learning them all over again, so I brought it down to a much smaller model. A piece of purple felt, silver ribbon and a few stones, about fifteen in all, in a bowl. It matters not that I choose the same stones each time; it's the placing which is always different. I have an 'I' stone which goes in the middle of Present and the other stones are put on the cloth with eyes shut. I read from the positions of the stones just the same, which section they're in, how they relate to one another, are they touching, are they even close, are they on the ribbon so they're crossing over from past to present or present to future, what is clustered around the 'I' stone, all this leads to the reading.

It sounds strange, it sounds random, but one time the Child stone went off the cloth and onto my desk. I mentioned it in the reading, as you must with everything that happens, to be told yes, the couple had lost a child.

There was another occasion when I created an even smaller version with just ten stones, which I took to Open Circle night. These were pebbles, they didn't look like anything; they couldn't convey anything to anyone who hadn't named them as I did. The person I was reading for put the Family stone as far into the Past as she could go without it actually going off the cloth. I told her she'd done that and she said, 'I haven't spoken to my mother in thirty years.'

The stones have never failed me. I know Redwood is there when I work; the readings are always in two parts, my reading of the stones; his strong voice from the Realms. They aren't done in a hurry, they take time; they take consideration and concentration.

There is a little book, Cast In Stone, which sets this out clearly for anyone who wants to try the ancient Mayan way of divination. Your guide will let you know if it's right for you.

They aren't done in a hurry, they take time; they take consideration and concentration.

That's a good description of my tarot readings. Just as my stones are different, so are my cards. It seems a good place for another side-line, does it not?

I 'found' the cards on eBay. They're a deck of black and white photographs of everything and anything, from castles to cars driving through floods, from games of tennis to a vicar standing in a wood. They're as random as that. The whole deck is made up of these vivid, sometimes surreal, sometimes offbeat photographs. Mahatma Gandhi, a window with water being sprayed at it, two people outside an old London telephone box, that's a few more. They have a black back with a white pentagram and that's it. No book, no instructions, I can't read anything to explain what I'm looking at, it has to come from spirit and nowhere else. All the seller could tell me is that they dated from around the 1930s and came from Canada. No one has seen a deck like it, one person I contacted owns over two hundred tarot decks but has nothing like mine.

My usual 'spread' is seven cards, one for NOW and six for the future. The last reading I did brought the response that he, the questioner, had never received a 99% accurate reading before. It's like the stones, different, as I am. We have to find the tools we need to work, and the tools can't be given to us by someone else, they have to be our choice, our instinctive choosing. If you work with crystals, you will be drawn to certain colours, certain types. Always follow that instinct, buy what you are called to own. It will mean more to you. It will stay with you and be an integral part of your pathway.

Onward… Ventnor church memories: a highly spirit connected medium, Tom Smith, was booked to come to the church for a service. He couldn't stop giving messages, walk up to him and he would start reading you immediately. This is a good moment to mention the things he said to me, as one of them was 'you'd be good with cards.' I remember I said, 'I don't read the tarot.' He said, 'any cards, playing cards, try them all.' Playing cards didn't work for me either, it was when I found my tarot cards I realised his prophesy had come true.

The other thing he said, which links back to an earlier part of this journey, was 'two children.' I said 'no, just one.' He shook his head. 'Two children, one here, one up there.'

I had been experimenting with psychic art, trying to draw faces. Most of them came out looking like stereotyped Native Americans but I drew a small boy's face three times - exactly the same. A boy. A son. The child I lost eighteen months before my daughter arrived. My son in the realms. I truly had miscarried and I think this was because my husband said emphatically he wanted a blonde, blue eyed girl. My son went back and has been there throughout my life, watching over me from the spirit realms.

As is the way with all things in spirit and me, my son is a clown, a practical joker. He's probably responsible for most of the strange noises I hear around this flat. The one thing I know for sure was he overheard me say 'wake me at 6.' I was woken next morning by a voice calling 'Mum!' I crashed into my daughter's bedroom to find her rudely woken by my rushing in and demanding to know what was wrong. I said I'd been dreaming, sorry. I went back to my bedroom, picked up the clock and saw it was 6 AM. Then I heard the laughter…

I mentioned my friend and spirit artist Ann Davies way back up there – I was 'looking' for a psychic artist and was busy scanning names on the Internet. Her name came up, it caught my attention as Ann (no e) is my middle name and we share the last name. On impulse I called her. I said, almost idiotically, 'I'm calling you from the Isle of Wight.' She said, 'I'm watching a travel programme about the Isle of Wight right now.' The connection has just grown stronger over the years. Give way to your impulses to do something, say something, write something if it's strong, it's invariably the right thing to do. This is also why I can't write in a linear way, my life progresses day to day, spirit are around all the time, pushing here, shoving there, events overlap…but by the time we get to the part when you get to do the work, so you can take over when I'm not here (LOL) you should have got all the essential parts.

Moving onward, in a manner of speaking.
    Ventnor church wasn't all smooth sailing by any stretch of the imagination, but we worked on, raising money, clearing loans, getting woodworm ridden chairs taken away and smart new ones brought in. We (Brian Rice was president and a group of us were the committee) worked with some

wonderful mediums, including David Millard from Gosport. Here again we found David wasn't widely accepted as he brought humour into his talks and clairvoyance. The humour was always directed at himself, the afternoons and evenings he came were full of energy and light but it was always that residual 'we must be solemn, we must not jest in the name of spirit' attitude which pervaded everything. A reading with David lasted twenty minutes, a short time; a long time. He managed to tell me all I needed to know in that time span.

This also brings back a memory of arriving at the church when David was due to give an evening of clairvoyance and were hit by an overwhelming smell of gas. I called the emergency number, told them it was a church, they asked how many people were due for the meeting, I said thirty, they were there in about a minute... a leaking gas fire had filled the whole building with fumes!

One memory of that difficult time was writing yet another letter to the SNU about the ongoing arguments in the church. Daniel was around a lot at that time, getting agitated by the nonsensical problems. I wrote the letter, closed the file with the intention of letting it 'sit' for a couple of days before sending, then thought of something and opened the file again. All of thirty seconds had passed, by my estimation.

The letter had gained an addition. Under the address of the SNU Daniel had typed

ALL HA HA

I didn't send it. I laughed and felt the whole weight of the 'problems' slide from me. Nothing there bothered me again.

Another memory is of overlooking the fact most of the 'opposition' to us were not as spiritually aware as I was, for one. So the day I rushed in, telling people I had smelled wet fur in my car on the way there, was an odd one, judging by the strange looks I got and the whispers behind hands. I was alone in the car; I drove to Ventnor in the rain and was very aware of that musky heavy smell only wet fur generates. I had no idea who was in the car with me... it was a good number of years later I discovered my animal totem is a red fox. I have since been gifted a wolfhound who also walks with me. His name's Teague.

Finally a group of us walked away from the church and set up Independent Spirits. Here was an even clearer example of the humour that consistently came through from the Realms. I had seen some elaborate and fancy names for groups, Messengers of Light, things like that. I asked spirit for a name and they gave me Independent Spirits. Straightforward, said it all. We were holding meetings in a local hall on Sundays, very successfully, too. Excellent energies, good clairvoyance, a sense of true companionship.

That ended when the council changed the rules for the hall use and we began meeting in a guest house. The one thing that stands out for me from that time was an evening with Derek Marney, a powerful and emotive speaker and demonstrator. He looked round at the audience and said: 'what am I doing here when you have three mediums among you?' He pointed to a male friend who always denied he was a medium, to my friend Mary and to me. It was the first time someone had in essence said straight out, 'you're a medium.' It was a spotlight turned on inside.

During all these meetings, circles, readings, I was growing in strength and knowledge. There is so much to learn, it would be easy to drown under the weight of books by Silver Birch, Ramadahn and all the other great guides who have come through with philosophy. I don't seem able to retain that kind of information, it slides by me and is gone. I'm saying this so don't worry if it happens to you, we can't all be walking founts of spiritual knowledge. Some are; those are the ones we go to for our information. The rest of us are the worker ants, building communities where others are nurtured and can grow. All I need to know about spirit comes from spirit direct to me.

Eventually the guest house location was closed to us, so we relocated again, holding meetings in West Wight once a month. Still the word got out through talented committed dedicated mediums who came to the island to demonstrate their skills, people such as Joan Shergold who brought psychic portraits to see if they could be accepted by the people attending and drew new ones in front of everyone, then read from the portrait once it had been identified.

As it happens, Joan said she had long wanted to be with someone in trance and draw whoever came through during the trance session. We arranged a

Sunday at Mary's home, Joan had her paper and charcoal and I had Redwood, Clarence, Antony and goodness knows who else with me for protection.

I slid into trance very easily, as I do at Mary's. Sometimes in a very small circle evening we would turn out the lights to see what we could see (spirit lights, energy spirals, people…) and I would go into trance every time without fail. This Sunday was no different, straight into another world of peace and total calm.

I remained in trance for three hours. During that time Joan talked with and drew Clarence and two other people. I have long since forgotten the other two and have only snippets of whatever it was Clarence said, for the trance was very deep and peaceful and I retained only the tiniest fragment of it. Joan was delighted, which was all that mattered.

One of the good things which came out of the monthly meetings was meeting Felicity Medland, daughter of the great healer Harry Edwards. It was suggested by someone we had Felicity as a speaker at one of our Sunday meetings. She is an entertaining speaker, having many anecdotes of her time with her father, especially when he demonstrated his healing in the Royal Albert Hall. For anyone who is interested, her father set up the Harry Edwards Healing Sanctuary. That afternoon talk has resulted in my visiting her every month ever since. During that time she has given me with three beautiful serene oil paintings and a series of needlepoint portraits. This is the reason for including her in this book: Felicity creates portraits of people from their visits to her. She must be the

48

only psychic needlepoint artists in the United Kingdom! If anyone else knows of anyone who can do this, I will be pleased to hear from them…

My walls are graced with her finely stitched portraits of Anne Boleyn, Jane Seymour, Anne of Cleves, Katherine of Aragon and Katherine Howard.

There really are no limits to the ways spirit will get their message across to the world. The message is, as always, we are not dead, we are here; we are waiting to speak with you.

There is no death. For ten years we held regular monthly meetings in Freshwater carrying this message to many, many people. We would be doing it today had attendance not fallen off, indifference gets to everyone in the end. The hall hire had to be covered…

So… there I was, doing my bit, sometimes giving trance addresses to the audience, sometimes doing ribbon readings or helping Mary with crystal readings, or my own clairvoyance and all the time knowing there were bigger tasks for me, there were so many spirits around me all the time I knew I had to talk with them, find out what they wanted me to do.

A quick side-line, I have just looked up, seen this and remembered I wanted to include it in the book.

I collect moons. My office walls are covered in them and there are many hanging from the ceiling. One is from a Charlie Chaplin film starring the Kid. He is standing on the moon; Charlie is hanging off it by his walking stick. This moon usually hangs with Charlie looking out of the window. Once or twice a year it begins to move, to turn, until it's completely round the other way. It doesn't move when the computer is on to generate vibrations so it has to be someone turning it, a bit at a time. I know Charlie is around occasionally, I sense his presence, I know the smile only he can give. Sometimes I see the flickering outline which says someone's here.

It takes a lot for a spirit to do anything, move something for example and as for showing themselves, that really does take some energy. Despite that, Derek Marney told me over twenty years ago I would one day see spirit as clearly as I saw him.

Hint to spirit… I am still waiting… patiently…

It does mean the powerful spirits get to do things for not quite so powerful spirits: that's just been given to me and makes perfect sense.

Something else I remembered and wanted to share with you:

I recalled another Happening, one that's important to tell you, because of the message it contains. I was driving back from Freshwater one Monday night when the police stopped me – they were doing spot checks on vehicles – because I had a defective headlight. They were looking for drunk drivers, so they insisted I used the breathalyser, which refused to work, much to their annoyance and my secret amusement. I was annoyed at being delayed at 11 PM when I wanted to get home, so drove off muttering under my breath.

I took the car into the garage next morning to ask for a bulb for the headlight. One of the mechanics came out to look at the car and said 'your offside back tyre is dangerous. It could blow at any time.'

If the police hadn't stopped me...

The message of this story is – everything happens for a reason, even if it annoys, aggravates and downright infuriates you. There's a reason for it. I recall reading a short item by someone who said she and her partner were travelling on the motorway to a place new to them. They took the wrong exit and found themselves in country lanes. It took an age for them to find their way back onto the motorway which was oddly empty. Later they heard there had been a massive multi-car accident between the two exits – they would have been caught in it if they hadn't 'taken' the wrong exit.

Hold back and see what happens... you'll find yourself thinking 'if that hadn't happened...' it may not be life changing but equally it could. Be aware that everything, every single thing that happens to us in our lives, is for a reason. It makes those annoyances easier to cope with, too. Think on my mother's oft repeated comment which is so very true:

Look for the good thing which always comes out of the bad.

I'm trying hard to remember to talk about my material life as well as my spiritual life, as the two things are so interconnected I can't separate them.

I'm dropping back in time to the five years when my dear friend Terry all but gave up work with the publishing company to take care of his wife Jill, who was terminally ill.

The publishing company closed when the internet really got going (it hasn't been there forever, it just feels that way) and three of us opened a second-hand shop. It became my day job. It's called The Old Curiosity Shop, despite there being another in a nearby town, because as we were arranging to take over the rent of the shop, Jill said, in a dream, 'The Old Curiosity Shop, it will be good for you.' There was no disagreement, that's the name we have.

BTW, the shop is in Clarence Road…

We were busy with work one day, about three years ago, I think, when I called Shaun to tell him there was a coach opposite and all the people getting off were in fancy dress. That's how it looked to me. In fact it was the Victorian Strollers in town for a visit. They came over to the shop and I was formally introduced to 'Queen Victoria.'

The Strollers come from all over the country, they are used as extras in films, they attend 'events', such as the Victorian Weekend at the Havenstreet Steam Railway, they go to Osborne House, do all the things Queen Victoria used to do. The costumes are authentic, made from Victorian dress patterns; it's always an event when they arrive.

They came again the following August. This time I had advance notice and created a special welcome window for them. We have a photograph, taken by the East Cowes Heritage Centre, of the queen outside with family and ladies in waiting. This tipped me into advertising the shop as being By 'Royal' Appointment. This in turn amused the Strollers so much they made a point of visiting us the next time they came to town.

Tourists comment on it, one day customers came in and said, 'love the name of your shop.' We're not unique in the name, we are unique in the shop, which is full of flowers, ribbons, 'not for sale' items which are there to make it more interesting and attractive than the average second hand shop. We want to live up to our name. Jill was right; the name is good for us.

Terry is no longer with us. Shaun and I run The Old Curiosity Shop of East Cowes and are making a success of it in Terry's memory and also for us: it gave us a focus which we needed after he passed in 2015.

Talking of Terry... I have been scrolling back and forth through the pages already done, looking for the right place to talk about another Happening which involved Terry as well. So, let me drop it in here.

From out of 'nowhere' I developed a longing to visit the Rollright Stones in Oxfordshire. I told Terry of this and he said he too wanted to visit them. He had often talked of touring round the Cotswolds, visiting places he knew back when he was a mainland person and so we began making plans.

Like all plans, they tended to go awry often, and it was a full five years before Terry bought a motorhome and said we were going to the Cotswolds and the Rollright Stones. I made wreaths with artificial flowers which he wanted to put on his grandparents' graves. This happened in the last year of his life. I am sure he knew he was dying and was determined to do everything he said he wanted to do. We went, we placed the wreaths and one bright sunny morning we went to the Rollright Stones.

We walked along the rutted pathway and there before us was the magnificent ring of stones. Terry was a good way ahead of me and I watched him stop in his tracks. He turned and said, 'I'm getting, don't go in the circle.' 'I'm getting' is pure medium talk… which I stored for the moment and tried to approach the stones. I got exactly the same message. It was like a huge energy field had covered the stones and deliberately blocked us from going in. So we visited the quite separate King Stone instead, which was much friendlier.

When we got back to the motorhome, Terry asked, 'how do you feel?'

I said, 'as if I'd just had an energy drink.'

'Me too,' he said and started the vehicle. The 'full of energy' feeling lasted all day, we both walked further than usual, for Terry this was a big deal, as his heart was playing up and walking left him breathless.

I never found out why we were stopped from going into the circle, I do know we both benefited from visiting them, in some way.

(*It's the 12th October 2017. I am thinking about our visit to the Rollright Stones and have just written that I never found out why we were stopped from going into the circle. The answer has just been given to me. The stones are incredibly powerful, if we had gone into the vortex of energy which they give off, Terry's heart would have given up a lot sooner than it did. We were stopped as he was not at his time for going home.*)

A side-line here, something I remembered this morning and wanted to add it. Terry said once when I walked into the room it was as if I had someone else with me. I do, but it takes a sensitive person to know that. He always denied he was a sensitive but would talk to me of footsteps overhead when he was alone, of his flashy gold jacket rippling as if blown by a stiff wind, of voices in his home. He was every bit as psychic as me but never used it, well not until the very last night of his life.

Terry's passing. After Terry became a widower, I went to the house every morning, fed his two cats, made coffee and got the biscuits he liked. I took it all into the bedroom and woke him up. This particular day I did all that, cats, coffee, biscuits, walked into the bedroom and found he had passed on in the night. I walked around in a state of shock all day, not really thinking. I made a few phone calls, including one to Brian and Shirley Rice. They invited me to visit that Sunday. We had a meditation, just the three of us. (Never underestimate how powerful three can be.) Almost immediately I slid into the meditative state and was back in that bedroom, only this time I saw Terry standing by the bed, smiling. He said 'good, you're here, I can go now.' To know he had waited for me to arrive that morning took much of the grief from me. It was- and is - a huge comfort. Not everyone can have that kind of experience, but everyone can take from this the fact that our loved ones know how much we hurt when they have to leave us and will find a way to let us know they're fine, fit and well and ready to work with us and anyone else they need to help, in their new spirit persona.

You will know stories where someone has passed, and a younger member of the family has seen that person that night or the next day. Younger ones have fewer filters for the spirit world to penetrate to let you all know they made the transition and they're fine.

This is also a good point to mention another very big Happening. Terry and I used to go to the White Hart at Havenstreet for lunch on a Sunday. After he passed, I started going every week, reserved table, a chance for me to be fussed over for a while and for me to truly relax.

Families tend to drift apart after bereavement when the central person, the pivotal person in the family, departs. I didn't want this to happen. The calendar told me that due to 2016 being a Leap Year, the anniversary of his passing actually came on a Sunday. I suggested to the family that we get together at the White Hart for a celebration dinner. This went remarkably well so we arranged to do it again the following year, this one, 2017. This time Terry's sister and brother-in-law came.

The first thing to mention is that during Sunday morning, while I was working, I kept getting, 'think big, think big.' I was thinking this related to the shop and wondered how we could make a small place think big.

When Terry's sister arrived at the White Hart, she said that when they came across on the ferry they saw a tanker with TERRY painted on the side.

I told Shaun about the 'Think Big', he told me that his son-in-law had booked the day off from work (with Asda) for the dinner, but had received a frantic 'can you come in, we need you!' phone call, which devastated him. Shortly afterwards he had another phone call, 'don't worry, you can't work anyway, there's no electric.'

No electric - just to the store. Nowhere else. Not the football club next door, nowhere. No one could find out why the store had no electricity…

Think big. It doesn't come much bigger than shutting an entire store so someone could come to an anniversary dinner for the great Terry Wakelin!

The week before this happened I dropped the shop camera, a Canon digital which I used for advertising shots. Shaun said I could have his camera and he would go home and find it. He didn't find it, he found Terry's Nikon instead. That is now the official shop camera. It feels right, far better in my hands than the Canon. It isn't all in my mind, I know that…

Whilst working on this book, I am putting together a collection of messages from pop stars, comedians and others, under the title Voices. I just found this paragraph which I want to share with you; it's another major Happening…

It is the 13th February 2012. I am recording now that on the 12th February Whitney Houston came to me, full of life and energy, sparkling with myriad spirit lights, to let me know she was alive and well. I have never been quite that cold, head to foot cold, in a car warmed by the heater being full o! She said she would be back with her message very soon, after I asked her to be sure to go for spirit healing.

The next day a friend wrote: 'I could have done without Whitney singing to me all night because an unhappy medium on the Isle of Wight told her to!'

I had not told my friend of her visit...

Living In The Past

How often have we returned for another life and how does it work? How often... an Eastern philosopher said that if the bones if all our reincarnations were stacked one on top of the other, they would reach higher than Everest. So, the person who told me I had lived fifty-five times needed a few zeros on the end of her prediction. I know, from Redwood's communications, we go back further than the current Mayan ruins, so it is countless years in the past. I also know the young woman who is currently narrating the life of a Cro-Magnon tribe was me, so there is 30,000 years into history minimum. Here go the coincidences again... my friend Ken in California, an online friend, writer poet and mystic, who shares much of my life, was my father in that Cro-Magnon time. He has added things to pieces I have sent him about living in the caves. The publisher of this book was the partner I had then, someone who has filled in a few gaps which Ky, my alter ego at that time, missed in her need to tell me everything about the clan and their spiritual life. Watch, wait, observe, see how the links show up in your life, who are you linked with in today's world?

It seems to follow, from everything I've learned, that every person we meet in our day to day lives were with us in our past lives. Mostly they were and are fleeting associations, being served in a shop or restaurant, for example, something as simple as that but then there is the stronger more important level, when you meet someone and feel as if you've known them all your life. Relate this to those who meet and instantly fall in love. They are very likely carrying on from a past life when they were lovers.

Sometimes the connections are on different social levels. One medium friend has said twice now that she was a messenger boy in Henry VIII's court, she remembers vividly how her/his legs ached from standing waiting in case anyone needed him. I was in Henry's court.

Before I had any real information on my past lives, I attended a regression meditation in Ventnor church. We all sat very still, I had never known such stillness, as the medium took us on a journey, down a road, through a gate, down a path, through an open door, into a library where the walls were covered in books, each with a date on its spine. These were the records of our past lives. We were told to 'choose' one book, as if we ever have 'choice' – we're always directed. I reached for a book, I think it was 1198, something like that, when it was taken out of my hand, put back on the shelf and a voice said, 'this is not for you right now.' I had to sit in the totally silent church for the half hour or more everyone else was investigating one of their past lives. I was not best pleased… but as with everything to do with spirit, they know best. They know us very well, what stage of progression we are at, what information we can absorb at any given moment, whether it is good to reveal something to us or hold it for a while until we learn a little more… it's all in their hands. They try very hard to make sure nothing disrupts that progression, which is the most important thing all of us go through, the better to take back to the spirit realms when life is over. So, although I was peeved, I knew enough to know if the time wasn't right, it wasn't right and there would be other times, other places, other meditations.

I had a past life reading done by Ann Davies. It revealed many things, my life as a priestess in Ancient Britain attending a funeral, the person being buried was my mentor and lover. It was Redwood in one of his material reincarnations in my lives. I know I was a Dutch sea captain who became a correspondent for a Boston newspaper; I know I was hanged for religious beliefs. I was scribe to Charles I, one of Guy Fawkes' sisters, a maid in Clarence's household… in one circle regression meditation I went back to Atlantis at the moment the tsunami struck, tearing me away from the lover who tried to hold me. Atlantis must be strongly in my psyche: I caught a trailer for a programme on Discovery, divers finding parts of the lost city. The diver was holding up a piece of battered stonework, the voice over saying they didn't know what it was, me saying 'that was part of the lintel over the main doorway!' as if they could hear me.

My spirit doctor is my past life husband from about four hundred years ago in Hamburg. I bore him five children, the last was named Magdalena for me; I was Magda. I helped prepare the potions and lotions he sold. It amuses me, even in the depths of my misery of being migraine sick at times, to have Antony say: 'do you want me to get your doctor?' and thirty seconds later Horst is leaning over me and saying 'Magda, drink this.' (The spirit side of me drinks the spirit potion and immediately I feel better.)

One Christmas morning Clarence said: 'I'm just going back to the Realms for your gift.' He disappeared and then came back with a person who was a towering block of lights. This was Olaf, a Viking who had come to the UK in the 4th c AD with his brother and taken me for his wife.

The story is; he and his brother were hunters. As far as I can discover from them, the Vikings landed on the Scottish coast, very unwelcoming, so hunting was probably the only way to survive. He told me it was a small boat, nothing like the pictures we have of later boats. His original home is actually Lapland. I found that out one day when walking through our busy town. A woman was taking money from the ATM. She was wearing a thick furry coat with LAPLAND in the design on the back. Olaf's booming voice was going 'LAPLAND! BEST PLACE ON EARTH!' with me looking round to see if anyone else had heard him…

Olaf was and is funny, solid, an indomitable fighter and guardian. He said he went out hunting and fell into a snowdrift. He didn't get out, so he died of what we know now as hypothermia. Because every woman needed a strong man, I took his brother Lars as my partner. Lars is totally different, quiet, learned, a gentle smile and gentle voice. Both are my guardians, especially at night.

One night I wasn't sure they were in the room, so I asked: Olaf? Lars? Are you here?' Two bangs, one on the wardrobe door, one on the bedroom door, virtually at the same time…

I bought a regression CD which took me back to Victorian times, to a street girl named Hannah who lived in Red Lion Court in the City and who lived her life thieving, serving, doing anything she could to turn a penny to her advantage. I have a half-written novel which has been in progress for over twenty-five years now. It features Hannah, a Victorian street girl who lives in Hosier Lane, directly attached to Red Lion Court… and onward… the novel centres around the London body snatchers, who laid the bodies out in the Fortune of War pub right opposite St Barts Hospital. When I told my mother this, she said 'your grandfather used to drink in that pub.' Links, links and more links. They are all there, it gets to the point when you stop saying 'happenings' and start taking it as part of the spiritual existence.

Whilst writing Clarence's book, I decided to find out more about my life in his time so I booked a regression session with the Island's leading hypnotherapist.

The results shocked me - and him. He said he had never seen a session like it.

I went back to Aragon, to being Katherine begging my beautiful mother not to let me go to that cold wet country where the sun never shone, to marry a man I would be sure not to like… hysteria almost, knowing it was no good, the marriage had long been arranged and there was nothing I could do about it. I rode out of the city and into the countryside to see the baked earth, the richness of the soil, the brightness of the sun, for what would be the last time.

Then I went back to Clarence's time and my life as Ankarette Twynho, maid to the Duchess of Clarence. Seventeen years old, with a huge crush on the duke, babbling teen-like nonsense about working for his wife but watching for him all the time and why didn't he notice me?

I had a second session to see if I could go anywhere else, but I went back to the same two people at later times in their lives. As Katherine I was pacing the stone floor of a chamber, my ladies flattened against the walls out of my way as I screamed and shouted and yelled 'why does he prefer *her* to me!' The total devastation was overwhelming, all the love I had for Henry was still there, would always be there. The breakup was killing me.

Then back further to Ankarette again, more of her life with the duke, still lusting for him.

To go back twice to the same lives had to mean they were important. The duchess died very suddenly and in his grief, the duke believed his wife had been poisoned. He accused Ankarette of the deed, there was a hasty trial, convened in an hour, and Ankarette Twynho was illegally hanged. It caused a lot of trouble between the duke and his brother, King Edward IV, too late as the girl was dead.

Clarence is with me to make up for the injustice of ending my life back then (and to write his life story).

Henry is around for Henry's pleasure and desires; I have now written two books, one from his viewpoint and one from the viewpoint of each of his queens, which he arranged. That's why Hampton Court was so vivid to me in this life and why the Wars of the Roses time appeals to me as a period of history.

Quick side-line, again, before I forget, we had a normal meditation evening at Mary's in which I went back again to being Katherine, this time to the wonderful moment when Henry rode into Ludlow Castle and asked me to marry him. You won't find that in any history books, but he's mentioned it several times, telling me what pleasure it gave him to do that. When we came out of meditation, each person spoke of what they'd seen, what they'd experienced. I talked about Katherine and Mary said that explained my ladies in waiting standing around, guarding me while I was gone.

And... Crystal at Silver Moon Psychics in the north of Scotland (one of the very few people I trust to read for me) said in one reading that her guide Thomas wanted to say hi, that he knew me from that previous life. He was one of my clerics.

Oh, and the time an email arrived from someone I did not know, referring to me as his Queen and saying he was 'my' Lord Fisher from Katherine's time. He later sent me a dream catcher, bound in red velvet, with crystals on the cords and huge white feathers, all fit for a Queen, he said. This person became the second biblical scholar to vet Judas' book. Everything is for a reason, whether it's confirmation or help. Turn nothing aside when it comes to you. It's there for a very big reason.

Antony Woodville, mentioned several times so far, is also from the duke of Clarence's time. I was his wife Elizabeth. We shared many homes but for me the best was Sandringham, not the one there now but the original building, ornate, elegant, our favourite. The other favourite was Newcelles in Hertfordshire. This burned down during the last war, I suspect due to bombing raids. I have a print of it, another ornate building. It seemed to satisfy something in both of us. This is the man I lean on day by day, who advises on the small things, wear a coat, take an umbrella, wear a cardigan you'll be cold today, regardless of how I feel in the house. Once outside it is always very different. He is always right. On things like that anyway... I remember being in a restaurant when he saw someone carrying a pint of Fosters to their table. His immediate reaction was 'I want one of those.' I said, 'you won't like it,' but he went ahead and got one anyway, then spluttered and coughed and said it was the weakest worst thing he had ever had... modern ales don't measure up to medieval ones, it seems.

Antony simply walked into my life. I had one of the bigger offices in the building when we were publishing, and was working on a book when I became aware of someone walking along the corridor and into my office, bringing a glowing golden aura with them. I didn't have to stop and think, I said 'Antony?' and as easily as that, he had come home. Back to me. We have shared other lives, ones we have never explored, the one we had then is the one which matters most, for some reason. I am wondering if our marriage was more intense, more wonderful than the others. It lasted eleven years before I died of cancer. This is not the place to go into Antony's history; along with so many people, he is writing his book. We are about half way through, or we were, before other books got in the way. It will be done; Such Is My Dance will be completed. It's too important not to be out there, it gives his side of the Woodville/Plantagenet discussion. It is surprising that, after all these years, there are still people who actively dislike the Woodvilles.

Many lives. Many people.

I am sure I was with Alfred, which could be why I ended up living near Wantage and saw his statue many times.

I know I was with Jesus as one of the female disciples the church consistently ignores or disputes, it helped when I worked with Judas.

I know I was one of Guy's sisters, which made it easier for him to talk to me when we wrote the book.

I was one of Charles I's scribes, which made it difficult for him to talk to me as he didn't talk to servants... I may well discover the others in time, revealed by working with those who come to write their life stories.

You will find your past lives coming back to you through messages, through meditation and through information. Example: I know someone who has never been out of England but who is fascinated with Mexico, Mexico City in particular. She has studied Google Earth, traced the city for herself, read books on Mexico by people who have moved there, it comes alive for her. How recent then is the past life which is calling to her? It happens with many of us, we just need to recognise it when it comes before our eyes and our conscious mind.

The question hangs before us: if I was Ankarette Twynho and Elizabeth, wife to Antony Woodville, then was I occupying two bodies at the same time? That would be the obvious question, but the answer is different... we do not actually live these lives in a linear way, starting back in history and coming up to today, we go here, there, all over the place. My Atlantis life may well have come in between Katherine and Charles I, for all I know. We don't know; we never will until we go home and explore all we have learned. It makes sense as a theory, lives circling round and back again, a brief life then, a longer one now. Someone said in an article on time, imagine a tape measure curled round on itself in a box. All the numbers are there, it's not stretched out in one long line. The numbers are touching one another and so, this is how and why we can live lives, go back and forth as it suits us, as our spiritual progression demands that we do, in order to learn the right lessons before going home. Again.

The big question is, why so many lives; so many experiences? Everything we do is a lesson for our spirit, experiences we need to have so we take that knowledge back with us. It's an essential part of our progression. Let me say here you do have a choice, you don't have to return to this side of life and live again if you don't want to; you are capable of progressing through the realms, although it will be slower. Some people are keen to come back and live a new life, others (like me) know when they're tired of it all and want a bit of a rest. I've been told there is work waiting for me from the other side, helping those who want to channel books from spirit. Makes perfect sense…

This book has demanded many notes from me, scrawled comments on scraps of paper which were then translated into a page in the computer, where they became legible. I freely confess my handwriting is appalling, to the point when at times I can't read it, but – I learned to type at the age of fifteen. I am now seventy-four. That's a lot of typing, a lot of keyboard work. I've tried voice recognition, it either doesn't like me or isn't fast enough to keep up, even if I speak slowly like a robot running out of charge. I get nonsense on the screen, so I might as well type it myself as keep correcting my dictation. What this means is, when writing, my hands don't/can't keep to the typing speed, so it all goes spider-like.

Somewhere in the notes it says, 'agreements before birth.' I'd heard this several times from the platform, when more outspoken mediums would say to someone 'no good complaining about your life, you chose it before you came.' There is a series of books by Robert Schwartz which goes into this in depth and makes perfect sense. An example is a young man, a talented athlete who suffered an accident and ended up in a wheelchair. In one life he managed to experience two different happenings, when he returns to the spirit world, he will be one step ahead of those of us who have chosen just one pathway to follow.

Think about your lives, what's the one theme that runs throughout your years? Lack of money, always? Lack of health, always? Lack of opportunities to use a fine mind? There is always one thing, one main thing. It's taken me a long time, but I've finally come to terms with mine. Being different, being an outsider, sometimes being second best because of it, when the 'normal' people come first. Being the one with the 'odd' thoughts, the 'odd' beliefs. People accepted me as a Christian doing my bit for the local church but once I became/ developed into a medium, most of them backed off. It's been a long time since I made the transition and I still can't get used to comments like: 'I've never spoken to a medium before,' as if I'm going to transform myself into some kind of devil, or entity, in front of their face.

(But then we did have visitors to the hall where we held our monthly meetings actually admitting they were scared stiff in case 'things came out of the wall.' Hollywood does indeed have a lot to answer for...)

It goes further. My spirit work, which I obviously chose before I came here, antagonises some spiritual people, too. Among other things, I have been told to limit my spirit connection to one hour a day. How could I channel books if I only have one hour a day? Charles I's final walk from St James' Palace to Whitehall took us three tearful heart-wrenching hours one Sunday morning. Should I have sent him away and said: 'I'm only allowed one hour?'

(Sideline, I edit horror anthologies in my 'spare time'. The conversation in which I was told 'only one hour' stayed with me. I set up an anthology called One Hour; all the action in each story took place within one hour. It worked very well!)

Others said I was 'too open', that I should close down. They don't know how I work; they've never tried to find out. Basically, before I get out of bed I thank my two guardians who have been there all night, then I greet my companions who come with smiles and nudges to get up and get going. We talk; we walk together until the moment I enter the shop and switch on the lights. (This applies to my earlier work as an editor, too.) The moment I walked into my office I would automatically shut down, because there was (and is) so much else to think about. But... at no time am I closed down to the point when I cannot hear them speak to me. Antony sometimes throws one of his silly comments into my mind, William Blake will come by to bring me news of my friend Ken thousands of miles away, Dave Allen will be influencing the advertising copy... there are always others around. As I write this, I am aware my office is full of people. I can see a mass of lights, people shaped masses of flickering lights that tell me they are all here, pushing, nudging, 'don't forget me'...

There are occasions when this 'being open' is right for me and I know now why spirit arranged for me to work this way. Our shop is built on the premise we are there to listen, do feel free to come and talk. We never say this but it's there, getting into conversations with holidaymakers, with local people, with those from across the island reveals many things. I am recalling the troubled lady who went through so much before she died far too young. We would talk of crystals, of spirit, of influences in her life and she seemed to find comfort from this. There was the man whose son committed suicide who came to talk, knowing he would find a sympathetic ear. The man whose wife had recently passed; he was aware of her and thinking he was going crazy. We talked for ages and no one else came into the shop while we were engaged in the discussion. Its accidental meetings, words said at the right moment, our ability to take on these burdens for a while, which tells me spirit needs me to be open to anything that needs attention and something can be given in return.

There are many occasions when I'm standing next to someone and feel the cold chill of a spirit presence run through me but can't do anything about it, as the person isn't showing any signs of being receptive to such talk. I have to keep those visits to myself.

Then there are times when I can say something... Shaun went buying recently. He went through the boxes the seller had ready for him and chose some items, then asked about the swagger stick he could see in another box. He bought that and found it had a name etched into it. He also bought a piece of trench artwork.

I advertised the swagger stick on a local selling site and had a call almost immediately from someone who said it belonged to her great-grandfather and her father would be coming to buy it. I asked if her great-grandfather did trench artwork. She said no, that was his brother who signed up with him… The artwork was the badge of the Warwickshire regiment, their unit which was sent to the Isle of Wight as Home Guard.

Sometimes you just know spirit is working hard. All the time I stood talking with the family I was going cold, over and over again. I told them this and they accepted it as totally normal and confirmation of all we were discussing. Sometimes it's just – wonderful.

All of us are called to work for spirit in the way spirit know we want to work. They fit with our needs, our capabilities. If it feels right, do it, ignore the well-meaning people who want to base your spiritual work on theirs. It doesn't happen like that and never will. The spirit council know exactly what they're at and will push, shove and generally create havoc to get what they want. This was brought home to me when a medium, during the course of a message to someone else, said 'spirit will even take you out of a long marriage if they want you.' That's exactly what they did with me. At the time it was hell, now I can't thank them enough.

The Writing Gets Serious

Exploring the world of channelled books

Living In The Shadow Of The Cross

Within a few months of finishing Daniel's book, I found I was being pushed to my next task. It was then I realised Daniel's book had been a test; could I write such harrowing material and stay sane? Yes I could. I cried a lot of tears (so did he) but we made it.

The person who made the critical comment about my letter in Psychic News made another comment which has stayed with me through the years. She said: 'spirit test us and test us and just when you think they're done, they test us again.'

If I look at the books I've channelled so far, I would say there is a lot of truth in that. Each book has been a test, some heart-breaking writing, some horrific writing, all of it needing to be said. I have - so far - come through it all.

Spirit are not inconsiderate, they know when we need a break, so my next book came as a delight, as I had done most of the work already. Archangel Gabriel had made himself known both at home and in meditation as my guardian angel and another clown in his own right. I was getting endless complaints about his wings, how much trouble they were, that he kept catching them on doorways and losing feathers… offbeat surreal angelic humour. He did say once he likes being around me, I don't ask him to be serious…

Archangel Gabriel asked me to write Living In The Shadow Of The Cross, using all the work I had already done as my foundation but writing it from the aspect of the angel who walked the earth plane with Jesus, the angel who was there at the start and at the finish. We did this, it took six months. It's a light yet in depth look at the entire three years, told with humour and great, great love.

It couldn't have been more of a contrast to Daniel's story if Gabriel had worked at it.

I asked a spirit artist friend to paint Gabriel for me. She said it would be a soul painting and take her three months.

No problem. The problem came later – 'can you tell me what colour his hair is? He turns up with blonde hair sometimes and brown hair other times…' She painted him with blonde and brown hair in streaks…

I went to Stafford to collect it, a long journey for someone who had always remained in the south of the UK. My friend said she'd had the portrait on her easel when two sitters arrived for readings. There is no name on the painting to say who the person is. The wife walked past and said, 'it's an angel, isn't it?' (There are no wings). The husband walked past and said, 'that's Gabriel, isn't it?'

It's a prized treasured possession.

He is a prized treasured friend and guardian.

He's a truly funny angel, too. You know this foolish 'love you' 'love you too' when family and friends sign off their mobile phone calls? He knows I don't care for it, so… one morning, ready to go to work, I looked at the portrait and said, 'I love you.' I immediately got back 'love you too.' I went to work laughing.

This is a good moment to remind you to say, 'thank you' and 'I love you' when you start work and when you are working with spirit, rather than take it all for granted. Most of the people you will work with were human once, they take human traits with them into the realms, including the courtesies of life. A 'thank you' now and then goes down well, just as it does on this side of life.

Death Be Pardoner To Me

Apparently it's a 'fact' ladies don't get hernias. That fact went out of the window in March 2005 when I had a strangulated hernia and was rushed into hospital for a life-threatening operation. Apparently it was bad, a three-hour operation to sort me out. I went in on the Wednesday and came home on the Sunday. Even with the speed of turnaround and demand for beds, that was as fast as can be.

My abiding memory, apart from the sheer boredom of being tethered to a hospital bed with more tubes and stands than any person could need, was the look on the face of the young Registrar who did the rounds on the Sunday morning. He looked at the wound, looked at me with shock and said, 'do you want to go home?' I said, 'do you want to believe in spiritual healing now?' He didn't answer me; he walked off to the next bed…

What I didn't know then but was told much later was I 'died' for five minutes on the operating table and went home to the Realms for five hours. During that time a lot of people visited me, including Redwood and somehow I was filled with knowledge and understanding, two very different things for me. (My daughter often said, during the months that followed, I had become more 'weird' since the operation. Confirmation…)

I certainly felt different, without being able to nail quite what it was. That glimpse of the realms, that time spent with powerful knowledgeable people, a hint of what is to come when I go home (none of which I now remember) changed me. I was already different; I became even more 'different', if that's possible.

July 15th 2005. I was having breakfast alone when someone sitting on the sofa across the room said 'Clarence.' I said 'welcome, now can you confirm who you are?' I felt a smile if nothing else. That evening I visited Brian and Shirley, a 'normal' evening, no circle, no nothing. We sat and talked and then, as I picked up my car keys ready to leave, Brian said 'can you take a George? Not your relatives (I have three Uncle George's in the spirit world!) one that goes further back than that. I can hear Renaissance type music and see people in doublets and boots.'

George, duke of Clarence, is from the time of the Wars of the Roses.

So, as I always do, I asked for confirmation. Somehow I felt I needed more than Brian's validation that night. I had, during the previous year, searched the internet for Clarence's biography. Abebooks.com, 110,000 books, no copies. Amazon, how many books do they have for sale? No copies. A specialist bookshop owner said if he had a crate full he would be able to retire.

Clarence asked, what do you want?

I said, a copy of your biography.

He said, file a request on Amazon. (I have long since got used to the fact spirits use the internet as well as we do…)

I said, done that and got nothing.

He said, do it again.

On the Sunday I registered a request for the biography of George, duke of Clarence. On the Tuesday, two days on, I had an email from a Cotswold bookseller, who had a brand-new copy for sale…

I said to Clarence, 'clever, aren't you?'

He said, 'smarter than the average duke, Boo Boo…'

He became Lord Yogi from that moment on. I've been Bobo ever since, too. Miracles, small ones, big ones, they can do it and they do.

I began writing Death Be Pardoner To Me, the life of George, duke of Clarence, almost immediately. I felt very strongly that we'd met before, not particularly in a past life although that revealed itself later, it was more recent than that. In a deep meditation I was told Clarence was one of the people who had been there during that five-hour meeting. He is often with me.

I should perhaps explain my titles. They come from the poems of John Drinkwater, a poet who worked in the early part of the last century. I look for a title that fits the person with the proviso that the poem has to fit the person too. Death Be Pardoner To Me was the first one I chose. Almost immediately I had people saying I'd misquoted, although they weren't entirely sure what had been quoted… no, it's a line from a poem written in 1924.

The book was complete, I liked it, he liked it; the task of placing it with a publisher loomed before us. I tried several agencies and publishers with no success. I usually avoid what looks like an online scam, but the ad which offered a chance for a book to put before fifty or more publishers and agents was too good to pass up. I thought about it for a time, then spirit said go for it. They did exactly what they said they'd do, get the MS before a whole load of publishers and agents. Nothing, absolutely nothing.

Well, that's not entirely true. It showed up the flaws in the publishing world beautifully. The publisher who asked me to change the end because 'it was too sad' – ignoring the fact it was true. Another said they only took fiction, so… is an 'autobiography' of someone who died over 500 years ago fact, then? There's not a publisher in business who would accept that! Then there was the agent who said, 'send it, historical fiction is hot right now.' So I did and she wrote back 'sorry, we don't take historical fiction.'

Word of warning to all who want to work for spirit, it isn't going to be easy to place the books, but -

Spirit were at work, as usual. An editor I knew well from past dealings called to say he was expanding his company's range to include travel, crime and anything else that came along. I offered 'alternative history' as it's generally known, and he said he was interested. I sent the MS. 24 hours later it had been accepted.

The editor came to the island on a flying visit to tie up loose ends, get the contract signed, all the usual stuff we have to deal with. Clarence and I went to the hotel – two doors away from where I live – for the meeting. Everything went smoothly, he said he loved the book, it was different, it was right, and I could feel Clarence glowing beside me. The whole thing had been his words, not mine, so the compliments were his.

We left the hotel, walked round the corner and into my road and then emotions took over. Clarence grabbed me and rocked me from side to side, like a big stuffed doll, while he had the biggest smile ever. He simply couldn't contain his happiness; at last his real story was to be out there. That was his moment.

Mine came when printed copies of the book arrived. I collected the mail from the Sorting Office, knew it was the books, ripped open the package and stood there with this book in my hand. Daniel's and Gabriel's books had been printed by the small independent company I worked for. This was 'real'; this was someone else saying the book was worth printing. I rushed over to a complete stranger, full of bursting happiness and said, 'I just want to share;

this is my book in print!' He looked surprised, then pleased, shook hands with me and went off with a big smile.

Brief and Bitter Hearts

I had been sitting circle with my best friend Mary and a bunch of local people (this is on the other side of the island to me) but the circle broke up, as they tend to do, and I got into the habit of going there on a Monday (circle night) anyway just to talk. We would invariably find someone coming to visit us. Sometimes they would tell us who they were; other times we played question and answer to discover the identity of our visitor. One night we had a powerful presence there, but he revealed nothing of himself until Mary went to make tea, leaving just me in the room. That's when he said, 'I'm Guy Fawkes.' I was to find this shyness was typical of Guy. He wanted to tell his story but hesitated to even ask me to do that.

I found a title, Brief and Bitter Hearts, set up the opening pages and waited for Guy to talk to me. Nothing happened for a while, then he tentatively asked if we could write the torture and execution scenes first, so he wasn't 'writing toward them'. They would be out of the way. I agreed and spent three harrowing weeks writing the truth of what happened in the torture chambers. I have very little time for accredited 'historians' who tend to borrow from one another rather than go to the available sources and, more than that, who don't seem capable of utilising an ounce of common sense. I'm saying this straight out here for a reason. In one

81

book on the Gunpowder Plot, the author follows the time hallowed 'fact' that Guy stood up and made a speech in his defence at the trial. Anyone with any sense who'd thought about this would realise it was/is the most foolish 'fact' in history. He'd spent four days being tortured. He was a broken man. He told me he'd been tied to a chair, so he was 'present' at the trial but that he was so far out of it he had no idea what was going on or what was said. To add to the nonsense of him 'standing up and making a speech,' he told me when they took him back to his cell, still tied to the chair, they didn't bother to undo the ropes; they cut them and let him fall to the stone floor.

For me it was three weeks of constant tears. I found it hard to accept the cruelty of the men. The torture chamber, the king authorised that, but cutting the ropes so the broken body could crash to the stone floor? The execution scene was almost worse, being dragged to the scaffold behind a horse, being pushed up the ladder to be hanged and then, the only light moment, discovering the executioner was a secret Catholic. He arranged for Guy to be killed, so he did not know he was drawn and quartered. I think I was on the point of collapse then. So, the interruption by Henry was welcome, for both of us.

I Diced With God

His Majesty King Henry VIII arrived.

My 'office' (my set aside room to work, shared with cat food and bags of cat litter and...) is covered in moons. They're all over the walls, hanging from the ceiling, on the pen holder, you name it, there's moons. About three hundred, I think, ranging from huge shop decorations and an equally huge moon with a witch sitting on it clutching a broomstick, to tiny earrings. Henry walked in, hands on hips, stared round at the display and finally asked 'what *is* all this, Katherine?'

"Moons, my liege lord, nothing but moons."

"Because?"

"Because I like them."

"Hm. Good enough, I suppose. Now, Katherine…"

'Now Katherine…' was 'will you write my life story for me?' I said I was in the middle of a book, but he said, with his devastating smile that helps me understand why women fell for him, that he would like to write his book immediately.

This resulted in Guy standing back for a while – not that he was unhappy about that, he was having difficulty talking about some things – and Henry's book started – immediately, as he wanted.

Henry was a fast and informative narrator. There are humour and serious incidents side by side, there's chat and there's absolutely no state secrets. He's more like a jocular uncle telling stories about his childhood. If you look beyond that, you get a very real picture of the man some people still refer to as a tyrant. Here are some of the reasons why he acted the way he did and here too are some things no one has recorded, his ongoing deep love for Katherine up to the moment he was bewitched by Anne - but was it real love?

To find out, you will need to read this book yourself.

Then we returned to Guy's book and I found what I had long believed, that he was and is a loyal, devoted, committed man. Once he found a cause he stayed with it. The stupid things people have written over the years are shown up to be just that – 'he called himself Guido' is one. He fought alongside continental mercenaries who used their version of the name Guy. Guido. How simple things are when you go direct to the source!

Captain Of The Wight

Google alerts are wonderful, type in the name and see what comes up as Google trawls the internet for you. I typed in 'Antony Woodville' and a whole load of material showed up. Whilst working through this, I began to see references of a disastrous campaign by Edward Woodville which took 440 men from the Isle of Wight to fight in Brittany – only 1 returned to tell of the slaughter by the French.

I had already tracked down a copy of the medieval report of a huge tournament Antony Woodville fought, big, showy, expensive, extravagant, rather summing up his life at that time… and wondered whether it was possible to find out more about the campaign, as no one seemed to know of it, but it was there. Very definitely there.

Google sent me an alert for the American Antiquarian Society Journal of 1901, which contained the original medieval report. I could hardly wait for it to arrive! When it did I faced a serious dilemma… the pages of the medieval report had not been cut. I stood, holding this ancient journal, with its uncut pages, thinking it would be sacrilege to take a knife to it but if I didn't, I'd never read the report.

In the end I cut the pages.

I had also discovered an Isle of Wight publication from the 30s with a detailed report in it – in French. It cost me a fortune to have translated as the initial estimate was a long way short of the final bill. Somehow I found the money and ended up, with Sir Edward's help, writing a three-part book (a small one) on the subject.

The first part is a fictionalised account of how the campaign came about, including a true saga written to include all the Island names of those who signed up to go. The second part is the translation. The third part is the original medieval report for those who want to read it.

I have asked myself why an American magazine would devote so many pages to a medieval report of a long overlooked and forgotten campaign. I asked the current editor, who said he had no idea why they would have included it, as it wasn't even American.

I'm saying… over 100 years ago spirit nudged someone into including the report, knowing that at some point in the future, this spirit of mine would be back on this side of life, writing, channelling, researching and generally stirring things up for the Woodvilles. The magazine could then supply the missing link. Local historian John Medland, here on the island, said he knew of the campaign but needed definitive proof to mention it. I provided that. There is no time in spirit.

Some time after my little book was self-published I found a copy of Captain Of The Wight, a truly romanticised account of the life of Edward Woodville from Frank Cowper. It was published in 1889, which says there has been an ongoing interest in the Woodvilles over time, even though most people say 'who?' I hold out hopes that Antony Woodville's story will captivate them. I already know his poem, 'Such Is My Dance', written in Sheriff Hutton prison the night before he was executed, has been set to music by an English folk group. Both Edward and Antony find this attention highly amusing. I know someone has written a modern work of fiction based on Antony and his sister Elizabeth too. The author got in touch with me, as Antony's biographer, then didn't ask any questions at all, so... I have not looked at the book... There's also a book titled The Merchant and the Knight, relating the relationship between Antony and William Caxton. There is more to the Woodvilles than many people give them credit for.

Oh, it's a good place to add this: I asked English Heritage for permission to place a plaque in Carisbrooke Castle somewhere in memory not only of Sir Edward, who began the work on the striking entrance gate to the castle (called the Woodville Gate until the early 1900s, when it became the more mundane Entrance Gate) but of all 439 men who never came back. Permission was granted; the plaque was made and is installed in the Carisbrooke

Castle Museum right next to the scale model of the castle. I was and am well pleased for Sir Edward's sake and for the many men the island lost at that time.

Thirty Pieces of Silver

This book came as a complete surprise, no question of it. I was meditating when Jesus approached, bringing Judas with him and asked if I would speak with him. Of course I would. He said many wouldn't… then Judas asked me to write his story. It was about then I was involved in Charles I's book, (another surprise, His Majesty is not known to approach mere mortals) but Judas assured me his book would not take long.

It didn't. Six weeks end to end, a chapter every night, three every weekend, every chapter going out individually to two Biblical scholars who approved everything Judas said. The only 'aid' I had was a DVD of the Holy Land, so I could see for myself where Judas began his life. Everything else was given to me.

The book covers the three years and details the intense friendship between Jesus and Judas, as Jesus works to convince him that he has to be the betrayer, he is the only one Jesus trusts to go through with it, so that the prophesy was fulfilled. Judas rebelled against it for a very long time, putting up all the arguments he could but his devotion to Jesus won out in the end.

It is only in hindsight we realise Judas is a very powerful, strong spirit. He knew what he was taking on when he came into this life, he was committing himself to two thousand years of abuse, hatred, misunderstanding, everything everyone would hate. He knew his name would become synonymous with treachery. He still agreed to come and he agreed, after nights of arguing, to be the one who ensured the prophesy was fulfilled. He went to his death with joy in his heart at being reunited with his dearest friend.

I was totally exhausted after writing a book in six weeks, a writing session that ended on the 30th December. It truly was thirty pieces – of tortuous writing and of joy at watching the true story unfold.

It was not long after that someone wrote to tell me CNN (Canada, I think) had broadcast a documentary which said everything Jude had said in his book. Confirmation comes in many ways; it's always good when it happens.

Jude is around a lot, he's a powerful presence, he now enjoys life and has a permanent place in my life, no matter which side of the veil I am on.

Fools and Kings and Fighting Men

With my past life knowledge of being Katherine of Aragon and the close tie I had/have with Henry VIII, I somehow wasn't surprised when he arrived, but Charles I really came out of the blue. I chose the title as being the three parts of his life. He says he was a fool when young, he liked being king but being a fighting man somehow escaped him. He relied on his soldiers to think for him.

We began well enough, covering the early days, his total absorption into the world of court, of finance, of diplomats – and of George Villiers, duke of Buckingham, who managed to lead him astray many times.

Then we began – or rather, I began to realise the work wasn't flowing as it should. I had some excellent imagery and some odd scenarios, but it was all stalling somehow. Then it stopped.

Ann Davies is my 'go to' person when I have difficulties. She lives in what she calls King Charles country (Stafford) and said yes, she'd find out why he was having difficulty talking to me.

The result was so obvious we both should have seen it. Charles, the autocratic king, had not moved on one inch in the realms despite many years of being there. He never spoke to the lower class, the workers; the minions. Quite how he brought himself to talk to me in the first place remains a mystery, unless you take it as showing how much he wanted his side of the story out there. Ann's suggestion was to divert from Charles all the way through the book and talk to those around him. So I ended up with the stable boy, his nursemaid, the doctor, his scribe, Queen Henrietta Maria, Henrietta's Fool, John Tradescant, Earl of Strafford, George Villiers, John Pym, Prince Rupert, Sir John Oglander (Charles spent his last night of freedom in Nunwell House here on the island, I went there out of visitor hours, much more peaceful and had a chance to talk with the then current owner) Colonel Robert Hammond, keeper of Carisbrooke Castle, John Cooke, Solicitor General … then my very dear friend Mary commented that the final part of the book should be open to Oliver Cromwell for his thoughts on the execution of his king. I was surprised how fast Oliver Cromwell came to me to give me his testimony, as we called these communications all the way through.

I had not written a book like it before, so many people; so many voices talking about one man – the rightful King of England. I watched him dig the holes he would fall into, knowing he would fall into them, watched as those around him closed the net that sealed his fate. And, as I have said before in this book, taking the final walk with him to Whitehall. It was devastating. He was only 49 years old, so much life ahead of him, so much to learn, to give – and it was all over.

Not The Shadow Of A Man

The life of the matriarch Jacquetta Woodville, not the one popularised in the book Lady of the Rivers. This is the true story of a woman so powerful if she lived today she would surely be in a position of supreme authority. Consider: she was married to a duke; she was a favourite of Margaret of Anjou and spent a lot of time at court, she managed to capture the most handsome man in England when a young widow (Richard Woodville) and produced fifteen children. Thirteen survived which, in a time, when infant mortality was the norm, this in itself is exceptional. She managed to make good marriages for her children, so she must have been overwhelmed when the young king Edward took notice of her daughter Elizabeth and made her Queen of England.

Jacquetta was a medium in her time, she was tried for witchcraft and was found not guilty, she suffered extreme losses as well as extreme highs.

She is an outstanding woman. The title reflects the fact she never allowed a man to totally take over her life.

The Darker Side of Henry VIII From Katherine to Katherine, Henry's queens reveal all

Henry asked one day if I would write the stories of each of his queens. He knew well I had begun work on Katherine of Aragon's story and shelved it through lack of time and pressures from other authors, so I said yes, I would, provided he did not interfere and let them speak openly about life with him. I also asked whether they had all agreed. That was when he told me he'd thought of the idea and visited each one in turn to make sure they were happy about the new book.

I began the book with the excerpt from Katherine's abandoned MS, which was a good start for me, a substantial amount had been written. In the middle of this, a distraught hysterical spirit arrived, shouting 'I didn't want it!' Jane Seymour had made herself known, in style, so I side-lined and wrote her impassioned and very sad story. Jane had been pushed forward by her family, more or less thrust under Henry's nose in many ways. None of it was her idea. The last thing she wanted was to go to Court as queen, to be on show, to be the mother of the king's heirs... the sad part is she did not die through childbed fever or anything like it. Her words are, 'they butchered me to get the child out. On Henry's orders.'

In many ways it was good to get that particular sadness written, which is not to say the others were any easier. Anne Boleyn was and is still in love with Henry, Anne of Cleves reveals that the annulment was false... Kathryn Howard, another who was pushed under Henry's nose, ended up doing a service for him which few would even dream would happen in that time... and Katherine Parr was, by her own admission, not much more than a nursemaid but she did bring Henry comfort and solace in his final years.

An intriguing book in many ways.

When it was done, I mailed it to my publisher, who immediately wrote back to say Henry had rushed in, as usual, saying 'I demand a right of reply to this outrageous tittle-tattle... even if it is true...' He is denied a right of reply, I had already told him he had his own book and had his chance to put the record straight, if he wanted to, in I Diced With God...

Work In Progress

Good Was The Day

The life and times of John F Kennedy. We will finish the book... he has much to say and an easy, readable style in which to say it. I've read his book Why England Slept, it should be required reading for all our politicians...

In My Troubled Season

This is a book I am most anxious to work on. It's the story of Elizabeth I and Mary. Queen of Scots, told through alternating chapters. This book is under way. I soon found that the queens would not turn up on the same night, even if I finished work with one, leaving sufficient time to get to work on the next chapter… two women with everything to gain and everything to lose from their association. It will be good, I know that.

Dispatches From The Mists of Time

These are combination books, a chapter per person. As William Rufus pointed out when he blustered in, no one's really interested in his life and times; they only want to know how he died. There's a lot of truth in that… the same applies to King John, King Harold, people like that. So, a chapter per person, starting with King Harold's right-hand man who is going to tell me how they motivated the men to march from Stamford Bridge to Hastings and then fight another battle.

One book will be devoted to **Powerful Women.** Indira Gandhi came to ask me about that one and I said yes, of course. Margaret Thatcher had already visited, so it was a very short time before she came to say she wanted to be in it too. Wallis Simpson (bringing a cloud of Joy perfume with her) also visited to ask for a place. There are a lot of powerful women out there, all looking to give their point of view to the world. They will be welcome, as soon as I get books finished to make way for them.

Voices

This is a massive work in progress which will see the light of day - possibly - when this book is done. It's a series of messages from pop stars from all eras; it's radio stars, politicians, all sorts of people who have come with messages for their fans/those who remember them. Some are half a page, some are longer; all are full of enthusiasm that they will be remembered in the pages of this strange book. Watch out for it...

Before Time

This is a narrative from a Cro-Magnon woman, Ky-el-Leron, the leader of a clan of cave dwellers. She doesn't know she is Cro-Magnon, that was given to me whilst working. It's a compelling narrative, using question and answer, full of details of the lives of prehistoric people most consider (up to now) to have been ignorant, half dressed, hairy, fur wearing beings who grunted at one another and spent time making crude tools yet somehow managed to survive bitter winters and baking summers. Every book I have seen perpetuates that image. In fact, when I mentioned my book at circle one evening, commenting they were highly spiritual people, one circle sitter said 'well, they didn't have much else to do.'

This book shows a different picture, it reveals a group of people with a structured spiritual society, one that reveres the spirits which controlled every part of their lives. Ky explains in great detail how their time is divided into two parts, Sleep and Wake, and how they utilised their days and nights preparing for them. The picture is of a society far superior to ours in many ways, everything is communal and yet each person is respected for themselves.

Such Is My Dance

The life of Antony Woodville, KG, Lord Scales of Newcelles and the Isle of Wight, 2nd Earl Rivers, dictated by himself. It's at times sharply sarcastic, it's deeply insightful for those who want to know more about that time and reveals an intellectual showman, one who lived and loved the high life of being in Court but who also longed for the quieter life away from all strictures of court, where he could be himself. This is half done, we will get there.

I have three channelled poems I particularly want to share with you at this point of the book. When things like this arrive, you have to believe in the whole spirit realm and the ability spirit have to do wonderful things for us.

The Rolled Stone to Dorothy Davies

Since

Since the time that you came
All the trials were the same
Since the time that love dwelt
Over the greyness in my years.

Since the time is of no matter
Since is only a word of no importance
Since means once upon a time
And time is on my side.

Brian.
Love to Dorothy

From Brian Jones
Written via spirit by Alan J Miles, 6/9/99

~~~

In October 2015 I walked into my beloved Terry's bedroom, as I did every working day, carrying biscuits and coffee and found only a body. The spirit had gone.

In February 2016 Ken Jones, poet extraordinary, channelled a poem for me. I have never known a poem to so completely encapsulate every single aspect of the friendship and love Terry and I shared, bound up with my life on the Island, too.

Hi Dorothy,

This poem came to me this morning on a beautiful overcast day. Somebody whispered it to me and said I should write it for you. As always, I am here for you in past centuries and those to come.

Sincerely, Ken

"I Don't Believe In Death" - Phil Yeh
Channelled by Ken L. Jones

I'm on an island I rarely leave
And once I had everything
Then in autumn I discovered
That it was time for him to go
To somewhere I cannot yet reach
Even though I more than sense its presence everyday
Now all my many friends share in my grief
And indeed it comforts me
But how can they exactly know all that I once had
And how it did fulfil me so

And now it's like the lyrics to a song
That cannot be sung anymore
But will always make me glad that it was born
anyway
On those long lost days
When I first found exactly what I was looking
for.

~~~

Speak Not To Me Of Ancient Days

Speak not to me of ancient days
Of ways that have no meaning in these modern
times
Ease thy mind in thoughts of now and not of
yesterday.

It behoves you none to stop and say
'It were better done in youth when times were
harder'
For in God's truth we do not see progression
that way.

Look now at what you have to behold
The glories of your world are manifold and fine
And all are in comparison like metal against
gold.

List now to those who want to fight
For better terms and cleaner homes where love
rules supreme
And men are prepared to stand for what is right.

Join hands with thy brothers in every way
Stand up for goodness, justice and compassion
in your lives
And look for the sunshine in every passing day.

We who are beyond the veil can do no more
Than bid you take notice of words which are
for you
But if you would but listen, then be sure

That your lives will be transformed and then
Happiness will find your deepest thoughts and
immortal soul
And quiet hearts and peaceful minds will be
given to all men.

William Blake
Channelled by Dorothy Davies

Closing thoughts

Life as a medium is fraught with emotions more than anything else. It's impossible to say to you, can you handle that? Because you will that find out as you progress. If anyone had told me 20+ years ago what I would see, feel, experience and live through, I would not have believed them. The sheer joy of being with spirit, the laughter we share, the fun we have – an example is my becoming aware those around me were busy with cleaning, sorting, tidying, arranging furniture, as if a Royal was about to arrive but then again, I had never known them to do that, no matter who was arriving.

Then someone walked in and it all fell into place, it had been a huge wind up for Bruce Forsyth's arrival for Voices… it's this sort of nonsense that ends up with all of us laughing and it's so, so good.

When the writing is flowing, when the words are there without you having to think about them, when the relief comes through from the person you're writing for that the truth is committed to 'paper' now (you may prefer to use pen and paper, nothing is ruled out when working with spirit) and will be released to the world, the feelings cannot be described. Just being with them, relying on them, having their friendship and love, is everything.

If this is for you, then let's move on to the next part of this book.

Are you ready?

Then let's go!

YOUR LIFE WITH SPIRIT

What's it like being a medium?

It's – challenging.

It's living two lives, the material one and the spiritual one and seeing how many times they overlap.

It's… talking to someone and feeling the cold chills going down the spine or, mostly, right through the body, the message that someone wants to say something and they can't, because so few people understand or would accept anything I said.

It's knowing there is no death, that we all live on after that moment of giving up this clumsy heavy ageing body we walk around in and being able to carry on where others are devastated by the loss. Knowledge gives strength and the knowledge that

THERE IS NO DEATH

Means we can look further than the funeral wreaths and words and know that the person has chosen a new life or chosen to help us in this life. Either way we benefit if we know it's happening.

It's - comforting.

It's being aware of those around me, those who talk to me, those who guard me. You will feel the same, if you walk this pathway, the one spirit have laid out for you.

It's knowing I'm loved and cared for, protected and guided by those who are bigger, stronger and wiser than me. You will come to realise how much you are loved and cared for too, as soon as you start work with your guides and helpers.

It's feeling 'different' and being grateful for that difference, for don't we all want to stand out in the crowd?

It's – exciting.

It's never knowing who might walk in and become part of the group around me.

It's being able to give something back to those who walk with me, even if it is only putting their words down on screen for them to read and revise if they wish. You will find your own way of giving something back, we all do.

It's getting confirmation of new arrivals and feeling that sense of exhilaration that they have chosen me. This is the 'different' thing coming in again and it's beyond description.

It's – confidence building

It's getting past the 'why me?' and 'is this real?' when people arrive to talk. You wonder if you're imagining things when singers, musicians, writers and others you admire walk in and start talking to you. Remember… they are all spirit now, all equal. You've been chosen by them for a variety of reasons: perhaps you shared a past life when you were both entirely different from the way you are now. That's a strong possibility. I know I shared at least one life with a famous person; we were torn away from one another when the tsunami hit Atlantis.

It's looking at others who might be scorning you for whatever reason – you know what people are like, you don't drive the right car, wear the same clothes, live in the 'right' area but – you have something they don't, determination, drive and commitment to the spirit world. So yes, confidence building, all the way.

Just remember never to say, 'why me?' They know why, better than you do.

TRUST.

All this can be yours. All you have to do is say 'yes please' and spirit will be there, ready, more than willing, set to overwhelm you with all the bouquets they can bring from that side to this.

So, shall we get started?

So you want to work with spirit...

I'll go through the various forms of
mediumship, expressions used, stuff like that,
so you have some idea of what it's all about
before you walk into it. Consider it armour,
of a type. There's more after this section,
you don't want it all at once.
Could be indigestible… (LOL)
Let's go…

There are different forms of mediumship:

Clairvoyance, clear seeing
Clairaudience, clear hearing
Claircognizance, clear knowing
Clairsentience, clear feeling.

All of these are ways of connecting with and talking with the 'dead.'

Mediums have one or more of these attributes as their psychic talent. Some have all four. I have all four.

There are different methods of divination:

Crystal ball:

The one image everyone uses when they write about psychics… a crystal ball can show you images, but it takes a lot of concentration unless you are one of the fortunate people who can 'read' from the ball immediately.

A quality crystal ball is expensive, if you want to go that route, get a small one to start with. If it is right for you, then invest in a larger one later.

Crystal readings:

This is a good one if you are drawn to working with crystals. They come in an infinite variety of colours and shapes, which can tell you a lot. So, you have a selection of crystals either on show or inside a bag. You ask people to draw some, preferably sight unseen, and put them in a small basket or dish. Take a look at the selection. You will find people 'choose' the colours and crystals they need most at that moment. Sometimes they choose all dark ones, or all blue ones, or ... you will see how it works. The crystals themselves, rose quartz, blue agate, moss agate, aventurine, obsidian, clear quartz and so many others, all have their own meanings and, added together, will give you a good indication of which way your message should go. Then you will find spirit moving in to tell you the rest. It isn't necessary to know every crystal, although there is a Crystal Bible for those who want to go deeper. What matters is the colour and how and what people choose when doing the readings.

Drawings:

Sometimes doodling with a relatively blank mind will reveal many clues to your needs – try it when your mind is full of questions and see if you get any answers. It's an easy thing to do. If you are fortunate enough to see a psychic portrait, you may find clues and answers in the way the painting/drawing has been made, the swirl of the colours, etc.

I Ching:

Extremely ancient Chinese form of divination using yarrow stalks or coins to create the hexagrams which are then read from a book. You need time to learn the ways of the enigmatic I Ching but it's worth it. Spending time calculating the hexagram itself is calming, even before you get the result and ponder it.

Ouija Board:

The spiritualist/paranormal world has many topics which cause divisions, none go deeper than the Ouija board. 99% of the 'problems' people associate with it are due to one place and one only... Hollywood. The board is a perfect foil for every horror film, the eager faces lit by flickering candles, the trembling fingers on the planchette...

Let's take a cold hard look at the so-called devil board.

You can buy one, plastic, wood, or cardboard. It will have printed numbers and Yes/No round the outside. You can put letters and Yes/No on pieces of paper and make a circle on a table. You then use an upside-down wine glass to draw the spirit who will spell out their message.

You can draw a circle in the earth... you see what I mean? None of this is related to the ghostly images shown in the films. A séance can be conducted without a board; when it is, the whole ethos of the evening changes, because every word has to be spelled out letter by letter. You can cut across that and ask the spirit if they would prefer you to ask questions and them to move the glass to Yes or No.

The board is completely harmless. It is no more than the wood, plastic or card that makes up the item. The planchette is nothing more than a piece of plastic or, if you go the paper/Lexicon card route, the 'planchette' is a glass you take from your drinks cabinet. There's nothing paranormal about that.

The essential thing and it is essential, is this: before you begin a session with a board, ask your guardian/gatekeeper for protection and entrust the entire session to them. Ask them to keep out all unwanted visitors.

You're now going to say, if there isn't a problem with the board, why do that? There is no problem with the board; the problem is with you and those who sit with you who are opening themselves to the spirit world. You could sit together in a small circle with no board; you would still need to place the whole lot in the hands of those tasked to guard you. That's as much for your peace of mind as it is for your protection.

A cautionary note here: always close your circle with a prayer of thanks. I have sat in two circles where there was no closing, the person running the circle got up and walked off to make tea. One was plagued with constant cold, no matter where she moved it followed and the other complained of darkness in her flat, of spirits trying to use her, of feeling uncomfortable, but not once did she close the circle. It takes a moment of your time to offer thanks to the Divine Spirit, to God, or your guardian angel, so do it.

Pendulum:

I have seen sites where they set down in stone, as it were, what a pendulum does when you ask a question. That's not good… first, you can make a pendulum, a crystal, a stone, a piece of jewellery suspended on a chain, all will work. Hold the chain lightly and ask, 'is my name XXXX?' Watch which way the pendulum swings as its YES answer. For me it goes right to left. Then ask 'is my name Dorothy? (or something completely different) and see what the pendulum does for the NO answer. For me it swings away from my body and back again, a totally different direction to the YES answer. Then ask something crazy, 'will it rain tomorrow?' or something as inane as that, a question that needs a 'maybe' answer and see which way the pendulum swings. My pendulum swings round in a large circle for a 'maybe' or 'possibly' answer. People get different responses from the pendulum; no one way is THE right way. Experiment, it's a fascinating and easy tool. Be careful about asking too many questions, though. The first three answers come from spirit, after that it is said your own Self takes over and you cannot guarantee the truth of the responses.

What it is very good for is finding things. 'Is the pen in this room?' 'Is the pen in this cabinet?' and so on.

Here I have the chance to pass on a little anecdote. We had a store room in the publishing/mail order building where I worked. Books and other things were left in A-Z boxes awaiting packing. I had mislaid a book so pulled out the pendulum and began asking where the book was. A visitor to the company happened to come in, saw me with the pendulum and completely freaked out! He ran out of the room back to the main office and almost hid. He used to stay – well, outstay actually – his welcome, this time he was gone in half an hour…

Psychometry:

This is something you can do any time, any place, to practice your psychic skills. Pick something up, a book in a second-hand shop is always a goodie, something that's been handled by other people, and hold it gently. See what impressions or vibrations you get from it. I remember picking up a very old very small stamp album and 'seeing' the owner clearly, a Victorian gentleman in high white wing collar, smoking jacket and hat. The huge cabin trunk we had in the shop told me it had been round the world three times. I got no more than that, but it was good.

And then there was the wrought iron and wood coffee table. Shaun was offered it as part of a collection of other items. He sat on it to look at the goods and felt something, an energy surge, go through him and the thought 'TROUBLE' flaring through his mind. It made him physically ill for a few moments. He asked me to sit on the table when it came into the shop. The first time I felt nothing, so thought whatever it was had dissipated itself into Shaun. When I tried it again later, I got 'free now.' The table came from someone who had just come out of prison having served time for violence. I wonder even now what it had seen, enough to impregnate the wood, I should think. (Shaun professes not to be psychic at all…)

Ribbon readings:

These are fun! You gather together one metre lengths of as many different coloured ribbons as you can, then attach them to something or tie them together in one bundle at one end. For my ribbon readings I sewed a loop of thin elastic to each one and then strung them on a large keyring.

You ask someone to hold the ribbons and then choose six of them, which they 'separate' away from the other colours. You get them back, you hold them, and you read from them. White is the Christ/spirit light, yellow for sun, green for nature, blue for sea, black for deep thoughts or unhappiness, pink for love, red for temper… this is all basic colour knowledge. Your task is to put all these individual attributes together and make a little reading out of it. You will be surprised how easy it is and how accurate it is when you've done it a few times.

Runes:

An ancient form of divination, an ancient alphabet, the runes have roots so far in the past no one can trace them. They can be surprisingly accurate. They usually come with an instruction book with complicated but intriguing layouts to try. I bought some but wasn't called to use them; they were passed on to someone else who was actively seeking runes.

Sand:

Asking someone to create a pattern in a bowl of sand and then reading from the picture comes into the category of needing concentration… but it can be done, and it can be very effective.

Tarot:

There are many different decks. If you want to try working with the cards, look through the variety on offer. It is said the cards call to you. You'll realise the truth of this when you go to buy a deck. You'll be drawn to one type, that will be THE deck for you and you will work well with it.

One of my quick side-lines… I was doing tarot readings through a website, we shared the money. I had to give it up because the sheer nonsense I was being asked dragged me down.
Questions such as:

Will my hair be normal if I go on using straighteners?

When will I win the Texas Thunderball?

What race and colour will my soulmate be and what career will he follow?

Should I go to Hong Kong and become a famous dancer and singer?

And the one which tipped me over to saying, 'enough is enough' –

Can I make a living from playing professional poker?

Reading anything, tarot, sand, water, crystal ball, whatever, is draining if there is no proper response; if the link is so tenuous you can't feel the connection. Those who asked these material questions were on a lower level and so I had to go to the lower level to try and answer them. I reached the point when I couldn't do that anymore. Ration yourself when you read the cards, they can take a lot from you until you're used to working with them. I remember going to a school fete and doing fifteen tarot readings one after the other. I left feeling like a washed-out dishrag and vowed not to do it again. The big worry is that the connection with spirit will weaken and you won't be as accurate.

Fully linked to spirit and full of energy, reading the cards for someone who seems to be accepting everything you're saying will make you feel good, both during and after the reading. The cards can be surprisingly accurate. Trust what you get, what you see, what you are given. That goes for all the methods of divination I am talking about in this book.

Trust.

Water:

There are people who can read from a bowl of water. This is called scrying. Like the crystal ball, it needs a lot of concentration.

***

Don't worry about any of this; as you progress you'll find your pathway, the one that's right for you. We all have different pathways and different talents. It may take time for you to find which one is right for you, the suggestion is, as always, try them one at a time, see what feels most comfortable and sits easy in your mind. What you are seeking is something to help you focus, whatever it is that will be the right thing for you.

Word of advice here – this is denied by some mediums but I have been told that to work properly you should not drink or smoke and give up perfume. The drink is obvious; you need a clear unfuddled mind. Smoking, two people come to me who smoked heavily during their lifetimes, I smell the cigarette smoke when they arrive. I don't smoke, I haven't touched a cigarette for thirty-nine years, so I am well aware of the smell when these men arrive. Perfume, this too I avoid as elegant ladies, especially those from the 30s, always come with perfume and some men come with delicate aftershave. It's best to be free of any perfumes yourself. It's a small sacrifice and will ensure you have a better connection.

We move on... to answer the question
What do you need to work with spirit?

An open mind/time

Trust

A willingness to listen

Trust.

An imagination, but not too vivid

Trust

Time to meditate

Trust

The ability to trust what you hear and see and feel

A level of sensitivity to others

Trust.

The ability to understand when not to speak

The ability to set aside all the scary spooky films and TV programmes on haunting of all kinds. It's rare to find a real one.

Trust

A desire to help others in some way, whether through healing, psychic drawing, giving readings or messages to settle their minds.

Trust.

Be prepared to be amazed. Be prepared for visions, for tingles, pushes, touches, noises, everything they can do to let you know they're there. It's easy to get over-excited and think it will all happen at once. It doesn't, so the first recommendation is:

Buy a notebook or journal and start keeping notes. Start by writing your memory of things which have happened, things which led you to think 'I'm psychic' – we all have them. If you write them down, you won't forget them, they won't get lost under the many new happenings and they will also show you just how far along your pathway you already are.

Be sure to write down everything that happens, any tingles, etc, any sounds, any smells or scents. These can be very evocative indeed.

Be sure to write the date of each entry. This is so, when you look back over the pages, you will see how far you've come and be surprised how much time has gone by. It will all happen faster than you think but not as fast as you may want.

This is a good moment to say, spirit know what you want to do. Spirit know how soon you can do it. They start you off gently, leading you onto the pathway they want you to follow, which you will find is the one you always wanted to follow without realising it. They know how much knowledge you can absorb at any one time. Think about it, you went to school for how many years? During those years you learned to read, write, do maths, absorb history, geography and heaven alone knows what else, often without realising how much you had actually taken in. This is why I say, keep a journal. When you think you're not going anywhere, when everything appears to have stopped, take a look at how far you've come and ask your guides, 'are you giving me a rest?' because they often do just that.

You need time to come to terms with everything you've learned so far.

Does this make sense?

Right, then we move on to the real work.

Beginning the process

If you can, set a time each day for your quiet moment, for some meditation. That can just mean sitting quietly, perhaps with a candle, and letting your mind drift. It's impossible for us to empty our minds, there are always thoughts waiting to creep in and disrupt what we are trying to do. So… let the thoughts come in but let them drift out again, don't jump on them and start worrying about every aspect of that thought. Just let it go. That will be a good lesson for you, a way to let go of your day's stresses and worries. Your stress levels should come down over time.

Allow yourself to drift through your thoughts. Do you see any colours? Lose yourself in them; let them swirl around your mind. Become aware of anyone in the room with you. Ask for your guide to come and make him or herself known to you. Ask for a name. Then let go and slowly bring yourself back into the real world.

If you do this regularly, you will find one of your guides arriving to talk to you, to offer you encouragement and advice.

Let me just say this:

When you begin work with spirit, you often have the wrong expectations such as, asking for help or a name or something and not seeming to get an answer. That's because no one is going to come in your room all light and brightness and loudness and terrify the life out of you. They can't do that, they won't do that. What happens is; they talk with you in other ways. Questions are often asked on paranormal sites about hearing voices, hearing noises, smelling something, doors opening and closing, things being moved. This is spirit saying, 'we're here, talk to us!' Small things, subtle things. If you ask for confirmation, always a good thing to do, again, look for it in other ways, feathers left where you wouldn't expect to find them, something said on TV, something in a magazine, something someone says, you'll hear/see your confirmation if you're aware that's the way it comes. A song being repeated endlessly which isn't on the radio, what are the lyrics saying, what is the singer saying, what is the group name... these are the things to look for and think about. They make us work as much as they have to work to get through to us.

When you get something, and have asked for confirmation, talk to the person using their name. Most noises, most disturbances, are spirits wanting you to take notice of them, they're not trying to send you screaming from your home. It's time to dismiss all that Hollywood spooky stuff and know that spirit work, on a daily basis, is the same as talking to your friends on the phone.

Be patient. Ask your questions and wait for answers. No one's going to be able to answer you immediately, unless you're very fortunate or very tuned in to them, as you won't be attuned enough to look for the answers at first. Patience, quiet understanding and looking for the signs they give you will reap massive rewards and you'll start your pathway seriously, knowing you and spirit are not just communicating, but working together.

Then you'll begin to see where your pathway lies. You might have expressed a desire to be a medium, to be a healer, to be a psychic artist, to be – whatever you want to be in service to spirit. They know, they hear, they're fully aware of what you can do and know whether you're prepared to do it. They'll lead you to the right places at the right times to meet the right people to help you do just that.

Nothing is coincidence. Nothing. Everything is designed to guide you where you need to go. Follow the signs, be happy with where they lead you and most of all, be thankful you're chosen. Thankful you have been awakened.

There's no life like it.

Where to look for confirmation:

Think about what you see and sense around you. Look for repetition and look for the different…

During my very first reading with medium David Marney, he said I had a brave walking with me who only had one feather and I had to find the rest. A few weeks later I got home from work to find a note from my daughter. It said, 'look what I found under my curtain!' A white feather. To get there the feather had to get inside an up and outward opening double glazed window and lodge itself between the glass and the curtain. She told me later it had been scratching at the glass... that was my first feather.

Then I began to find them everywhere. Not in the street, where you expect to find feathers, but in odd places, at the top of a flight of ten steep stairs, (the door at street level was always shut), under my windscreen wiper when it hadn't been raining so they hadn't been used, under my desk, all sorts of odd places where feathers should not be.

It got stranger after that, if that's possible. A medium arrived at a meeting with a carrier bag of feathers. 'They were all over my garden,' she said. 'I knew they were for you.' I counted them later, there were thirty-seven. I had just begun the Circle of Light so I said to spirit, 'you're three feathers short. The magazine has forty pages.' Two weeks after that David Millard came for the afternoon service. He pulled three feathers out of his pocket and said, 'these are for you.'...

I went to circle one night and found a feather propped up against the step.

I visited a friend and was given a cellophane envelope full of deep red feathers from someone's parrot. She didn't know I collected feathers.

One was stuck to the wheel arch of my car and stayed there for miles.

A parcel of books arrived at the office. In between them was a small white feather.

All these feathers are arranged in a box frame in my study and are added to from time to time, when spirit give me more feathers. They come if I'm about to make a spiritual step forward or I've made a spiritual step forward, a physical tangible sign that really sets the mind at rest.

There was one very dramatic time when my daughter and I were walking across the big car park near our home. It was a day with a perfectly clear blue sky, no birds could be heard, but suddenly there was a shower of feathers. My daughter looked everywhere, asking "where did they come from?"

Each of us works with spirit in different ways; your signs could be completely different. Look for repeating words, numbers, nudges, pushes to do something, always the same something, then you'll know they're there.

There's so much comfort in that feeling.

Your next move

Your next step is to find a local group, or church, and ask if you can join their development circle. You may well find that after two-three visits you don't feel comfortable with them and have to leave. This isn't your fault, it's the fact that you need to be of one accord to sit in a circle and benefit from it, if you or they are not in harmony, something will drive you or them out. It happens a lot. Circles form, do well, break up, re-form with different people joining in, an ongoing metamorphosis which is typical of spirit energy.

When you do start sitting circle, no matter where or with whom, remember you must go unless you've a very good reason not to. Think of it as an appointment with spirit. They're waiting for you; you need to be there for them. Everyone else in the group needs to feel the same way. It's when that changes the circles break up and re-form somewhere else.

The circle in the local church charged a very small fee, 20p at the time, to help with the electric we were using. Home circles often like you to take something, biscuits perhaps, anything that contributes to the after-circle tea. I used to take tea or sugar to help out. Check politely before going so you're not the only one empty handed!

Your guides and helpers need to contact you. They may well come in the meditation, once you relax enough to go on the journey set out for you. Quick aside, if you can't follow the journey, or your mind takes you somewhere else entirely, go with it. What matters is that time of total peace and you losing touch with your physical body and allowing yourself to drift into some other time and space so your people can come and talk to you. Sometimes you may not remember everything that's said, or you think you don't, but it will come back later. Another thing is, don't let anyone tell you anything you do or see is 'wrong.' There is no 'wrong'. As I said, we all work with spirit in different ways.

I vividly remember sitting a very tight closed circle with someone who had a Sai Baba shrine in the room where we sat. (Check him out!) and who wanted us to create a spiral of energy before we began. It was powerful, there were strong energies in the room; there was no argument about that.

On three consecutive circle nights I went to the same place, an underground cavern where my teacher waited for me. The circle leader got very annoyed at this and told me it was wrong to keep going to the same place. She wanted me to go off into the Universe somewhere, I believe. The fact is, my teacher needed to talk to me and she chose to draw me to her, using the energy we created. There was nothing 'wrong' about it. Apply logic to what seems illogical, it's surprising how well that works.

Then as you learn more, attempt more things, as you ask your people what your pathway is, you will find you are drawn to something which may surprise you.

Family Matters

An important topic which has been on my mind a lot this week: how your family and friends react to your opening up to spirit will set the tone for your future work.

I had a particularly vivid dream not long after all this began to open up for me. I dreamed of my beloved grandmother, who was handing me a copy of my favourite photo of her – one I had taken years earlier.

When I told my mother about the dream, she said, 'if your Nan's there with you, you'll be fine.' So… before you think this can't happen, or it has happened, and you don't know if it's right, your family members who are already on the other side are ready and willing to work with you and reassure you. For many people there's comfort in working with someone you know, someone you loved when they were here. If they only stay around for the early stages of your development, it is enough, it bridges that difficult time when you – in essence – declare yourself to be different.

Everyone has the ability to be psychic, some more than others and that is the group which often goes on to develop into the mediums and healers we need. Others are fully aware of their ability but refuse to go along with it, fearful perhaps, lack of confidence possibly, or a variety of other reasons. You are one of the stand-alone different people: you're reading a book which will help you become that 'odd' one who wants/needs to work with the spirit world.

So, your journey begins with your guardian, your family, your main guide. From here on out it just gets better, deeper, more interesting, more loving. You will begin to feel the love that radiates from those around you. You will begin to sense their presence and perhaps work out how you 'see' them. I see flickering lights or movement. Someone made the analogy that it's like the Stealth bomber passing over, the air is displaced, there is a sense of something and then it's gone. Don't pressure yourself with this point; it will happen as naturally as your opening to spirit will happen, day by day, step by step, moment by moment. It's like trying to remember something, forget it and it comes to mind. Don't worry yourself with spirit details; they will all happen when the time is right and more than that, when YOU are right. Remember, spirit know you better than you do. They will work at the pace which they know suits you best. You will be given time to assimilate all the new information, the new gifts, the new YOU.

It comes back to that same word, doesn't it?
TRUST.

Then there are the other ways of serving spirit:

Absent Healing:

Healing is part of the spiritualist movement and the life of a medium. You never know when you might be asked to 'put someone on your healing list.' So, what it is and how does it work?

You acquire a notebook, a special one preferably, mark it as your Absent Healing Journal and write your name at the top of the first page. Then add the names of everyone who you know could do with some kind of healing, whether it be physical or simple quietening of the mind. Look at the list daily, add who needs to be added but never take anyone off. You ask the realms, your guardian angel, God, whoever it feels right for you to talk to, to heal these people if it is in line with the Divine Plan.

No one can interfere with another person's life without permission. By asking for help and healing for friends and family and for yourself, you give that permission and heavenly healing can go out to those people – and you.

Later, if you are called, the right organisation and tutor will come along and you can become a qualified healer. Some organisations teach hands-on healing, (which I was taught) or a therapy where the hands are within touching distance but are working more on the aura and the vibration of the person who needs healing. Both are effective.

It has been said that the gift of healing is the greatest gift any human is fortunate enough to be given.

Auras:

Leading on from the healing section, everything which includes any natural material radiates its own vibration and, with practice, can be seen. Example, rose quartz has a blue aura and is beautiful. People have auras and, over time if you can see them, you will learn to 'read' them, to see where they may have health problems, aches and pains, headaches, that kind of thing, or whether their mood is depressed or full of sunshine. With that knowledge you can say the right thing at the right moment and make their day a little brighter.

Automatic writing:

This is sitting quietly with paper, or notepad and pen, and allowing spirit to take over and write for you. Automatic writing is usually entirely different from your own handwriting and if you channel more than one person, the writing will be different in each case. This is another method of channelling with the added fact that the handwriting shows it not to be you. You will know if you are led to do this, the compulsion will be strong to sit with pen and paper and just see what happens.

Channelling:

Writing the words spirit give the person channelling for them. Brian Rice works closely with a Native American, Grey Bear, who has dictated so many communications they fill eleven (slim but full of philosophy) books. The compulsion is to write, sometimes my fingers tingle; sometimes it's just a pushing sensation, a 'get going' feeling. It's unmistakable. It's automatic writing without the physical pen being moved and the handwriting being totally different. Now we use computers, they are very happy, the work gets done twice as fast... as you will see later in the book.

I have been working on a collection of messages from famous people and come across a comment which I wrote some years back and would like to share with you. It comes back to the 'it's my imagination' bit, combined with 'why me?' This is important when you talk with someone who is very well known and you think, if you tell people they are there, you will be laughed at, so it has to be imagination.

When someone goes to the Realms they lose their physical ailments, the ones that caused them to pass, but they do not lose their heartache, their phobias or their problems. (one of my companions has retained his phobia about spiders, but that will take a lot of eliminating. How many of us share that???) The problems are for us here to work with as well as them, it's our chance to do something in return for the great love we receive and the trust they place in us. They could so easily come and be laughed at, ignored, scorned or told to go away. If we were treated so, we would be angry and hurt and they are, too. They trust us and rely on us and we in turn should trust and rely on them. It's a partnership; not a one-way street. Trust is a two-way thing. Love is a two-way thing. We should not just take. We should give something back. I give my team all my unconditional love. I worry about them, constantly ask if they are all right, make sure they have somewhere to live, somewhere they can call home, something to do, to keep them busy and restore self-esteem and most of all, make them welcome in my home and my life any time they want to be there.

My reward is their friendship, their love, their laughter and their companionship. Never be afraid to say 'welcome' and accept whoever it is into your spirit life.

Circle, what it is and what it does:

A circle is a group of like-minded people who sit literally in a circle, with a leader who leads everyone into meditation. That means taking us on a journey into our imagination. For example, the leader might say 'you are walking along a beach under a blue sky. The water is gently rolling in. Ahead you see some palm trees, you walk to them, sit down at their base and look out at the blue sea. After a little while someone comes to sit with you…'

That's the magic of circle. It's the visitor, the one who comes in your meditation to bring you comfort, advice perhaps, guidance on your spiritual journey and possibly a message, who is the key to your continued progress. It isn't the same person who comes each time; different guides come in with different information.

The combined energy of the sitters enables healing to go out to all who need it. This energy goes into the spirit world and strengthens the contact between the two worlds. It is very important work for those on both sides.

When the meditation is over, and everyone has returned from their 'adventure' and recited it to the other sitters, the leader often goes into trance and a guide comes through to speak to the sitters. More advice or spiritual philosophy. This is often tape recorded, so the medium/leader can hear what was said, otherwise they miss out on it all.

Circles are valuable; an integral part of a medium's training. If the circle is 'closed', not an 'anyone welcome' circle often held in the church hall, you have to be invited to sit. The balance of sitters is vital to the success of the group.

If invited to sit in circle, remember and observe the courtesies. Always be on time. Always take a small offering with you, biscuits or something, to contribute to the 'after' time when tea is made and food circulates. It's another part of the circle companionship, taking food and drink together afterwards.

Circles are fluid, they change without anyone realising they're contributing to change. Sometimes they break up for no apparent reason, new ones form, sometimes smaller groups. Home circles are often more intense and get better results from the spirit world than the somewhat impersonal church development circles. This is something I've observed over the years. I think spirit prefer the more informal atmosphere of a home.

A quick side-line here:

Sometimes someone doesn't come to circle for whatever reason, and they don't let the circle leader know, they just don't turn up. That means there's an empty chair. By the time the circle ends, someone has come and taken that chair… it happens every time.

Energy:

You'll hear this a lot. It's all energy, us communicating with the spirit world, they using their energy to communicate with us. So, what is this energy? Try holding your hands about 12" apart and then slowly, very slowly, bring them together. As soon as you start you will feel tingling, it gets stronger and stronger until it's almost an effort to bring the hands together. Energy, your energy, is powerful. Imagine then a circle of people, a church full of people, all bringing that energy with them. It can be extremely exhilarating.

Everything has an energy. In the summer, try cupping your hands around a flower at the time when it is at its peak of perfection. Don't touch it, just put your hands gently around it. See what you can feel. Every flower gives off a different vibration, a different energy. It cannot be mistaken. Once you realise how strong this energy is, all the things we've talked about will make sense to you.

It takes a lot of energy for spirits to show themselves to us if we're not the lucky ones who see them all the time. When you ask to see someone, remember they may not be able to do it, for that reason. It's not that they don't want to…

Guides, who they are and what they do:

Guides are spirits tasked with looking after us on our earthly journey. When we start our work as servants of spirit, we usually have a guide with us who is used to working with newbies. Later, when we mature as mediums, the guide may change to one who specialises in working with people whose chosen pathway suits the one they had when they were on this side of life.

We usually have more than one guide: we have a gatekeeper or doorkeeper, whose job it is to keep away the undesirable types who may target you as someone who is vulnerable because they are new. It doesn't happen very often, it will never happen if you protect yourself. This can be whatever suits you best, a psychic robe that covers you from head to foot and shows no part of you, or a huge bubble of pure white light that keeps you safe. You will find your own form of protection as you progress. Meantime your gatekeeper is a guide to get to know and trust. If we get involved in healing, an experienced healing guide will come and work alongside you. There is also your guardian angel, the one who keeps you safe so you can do your work for spirit. They won't stop you having the occasional mishap or illness, sometimes we need these things to slow us down or teach us lessons, but on the whole they will take good care of you.

The great guide Ramadahn says working mediums have seven guides. I can go with that.

I read a story some years ago about a lady who asked her guardian angel to take care of her on her journey. She was involved in a head on crash; she walked away from the car unhurt. Later when she complained, her angel said she hadn't asked for the car to be protected, just her and that's exactly what they did!

Choose your words wisely when you make a request of your guides… (LOL)

When you go on meditation journeys, you may well discover the connection between your main guide and you. This is always interesting and adds depth to the relationship.

Working with Guides:

If everyone knew how good it is to work with guides, someone to turn to any time of the day or night and ask for advice, there'd be a lot more spiritually minded people. A guide is a spirit who chooses to walk with you throughout your life. You can ask them anything, should I buy this/go there/eat this (if you have food related problems they are a great help!) as well as life changing things, moving, relationships with family, there is nothing they can't help you with. Everyone has a guide from the moment they arrive in this life, so there's nothing they don't know about the person they walk with and nothing anyone needs to hide from them. Not everyone chooses the spiritual pathway, but then, the thought emerges, not everyone is meant to. I recall a medium saying sometimes we have to live a life without spirit, just to appreciate them more when we have a life with them. That too makes sense.

Most people look to Native Americans as being their guides and it's true they're imbued with great wisdom. Give this some thought, though, would it not be a mistake to dismiss other nationalities who may come to us?

There are the very wise and ancient Egyptians. The great trance medium Ursula Roberts channelled the guide Ramadan for many years; his Lectures are fascinating and fill many volumes. His mummified body is in the British Museum, she went to visit and sensed his presence. There's one guide which can be verified as someone who once lived.

There are the Chinese guides, bringing oriental wisdom to today's world.

Zulus walk with us too. How many generations of Zulus have walked the earth plane? Their strength is there for us as much as their wisdom.

Vikings, Europeans, Russians, British… even aliens, if you can recognise them when they come, all walk with us.

Who you walk with depends very much on the work you do. This life has been devoted to writing, for the most part, so those who walk with me now are writers, Antony Woodville, Sir Winston Churchill, Thomas More…

The one thing I want to get over to you is, don't be surprised by who comes. They were all human once (apart from the aliens, of course) and understand the many trials and tribulations we suffer on a daily basis. They are there to help, to guide, to uplift, to advise and most of all, to love us so we are never ever alone.

My main guides have been with me forever, others have come and gone. Cardinal Thomas Lindenwood came for a while, went away for whatever reason, no doubt for spiritual progression of some kind, then returned a few years later. My first guide, a Mandarin named Hi-Lee, specialised in working with newbies, so once I had reached the first level, he stood aside and Redwood was introduced to me. Although he had been there from the start, he hadn't taken any part in my early progression; he waited until I was on a higher level before coming in.

Our guides will do anything for us. In return they expect respect, devotion and friendship from us, which is fair enough. They give up their progression in the spirit world to walk with us, for some it's part of their progression but they would move on much faster without us…

I'm making a point of telling you this because when you begin your work you may find yourself 'losing' a much-loved guide. It's their karma, their progression, as much as yours; it's something us mediums have to live with. Trust me, it all works out fine. It's just the transition can be a tad painful until you settle down with your new guide(s).

Mediums and psychics:

A medium can and often does link with those in the spirit world, literally talking with the dead. A medium can use tarot cards or some other form of divination to assist in their connection, but it is usually one person talking to another, on this side of life, bringing messages from the other side of life. To avoid the ever-present taunt of cold reading someone, readings are often given long distance, by telephone, by email, so the person cannot be seen and nothing can be read from their expression.

A psychic uses cards, crystals and just about anything else they have learned to work with to bring the messages through. Either/or, with a good reader good information can come through.

Past Lives:

A huge subject that will take up some space, so for now let me summarise the subject as best I can – we have all lived many times before, living lives of richness or poverty, of good health or disablement, of dying young and dying old… there are many, many life lessons to learn and each time you return to the spirit world, you take back with you all you have discovered in your time here. This is added to your store of knowledge until the day you say all wrongs have been righted, all lessons learned and you need not return, you will continue your progression in the spirit world. None of us ever stop learning…

There are several ways of exploring your past lives. You can buy regression CDs (they work, more on that later) have regression meditations in circle (they work) have a past lives reading with a medium who specialises in accessing the Akashic records (the books where every single thing you've ever done is written down and stored) which I have had, or, as I did one time, go to a hypnotherapist.

Then you know it can't be faked, he would see through it.

Psychic art:

There are spirit or psychic artists who draw portraits of those who come to give evidence of survival through the magic of their portrait. There's nothing more evidential than holding a drawing of someone you knew or someone whose photograph you have, knowing it has come through someone who never met them. Some artists work alone, giving messages – clairvoyantly – while they draw. Others work alongside a medium who gives messages from the drawing itself and/or the person being drawn. I have a folder full of psychic art as well as a framed portrait of my guardian angel. (I can't draw.)

Protection:

We all need protection, even though we have our guides and guardians with us. A lot of the protection is for our peace of mind as well as being an actual happening. Imagine yourself in a bubble of pure white light encasing every part of you. That is one sure way of keeping unwanteds at bay. Another is to imagine a psychic cloak covering all of you, including your face and hands, and get into the habit of dropping this cloak over you when you begin any psychic/spiritual work and taking it off again when you're through. If using the Ouija board, imagine a ring of pure gold around the entire room, even the house where you are, let it grow and expand to cover all of the building.

There is one guide I need to mention, that's your doorkeeper or gatekeeper, depending on which book you read. This guide is there to do just that: make sure unwanted spirits don't come close to you. The Egyptian guide Ramadahn insists this is the most important spirit you have with you and that it is a good thing to get to know them well, to walk and talk with them, become close friends, then you know you can rely on them.

You will find your own protection routine and after a time, it will become second nature to drop into it. Be sensible, be protected.

Readings:

The word 'reading' is somewhat misleading. What happens is a person who needs or wants information from the spirit world consults a medium or psychic, depending on their need, and that person supplies such information as they are given by the spirit world. It's not very different from my standing on the platform of a church and giving clairvoyant messages to a member of the congregation, other than it's a good deal more private, one to one, and can go on for up to ¾ of an hour.

This is a good place to slide in a caution: when visiting a medium or psychic for a reading, be careful not to answer questions that would give information away, yes or no is usually enough and be careful not to 'feed' the medium, giving them information before they give the information to you. This applies to messages from the platform, too. It's very easy to say, 'yes I can take the name Janet, that's my father's sister and she...' that's for the medium to tell you, not for you to tell them, how else will you know the information is accurate?

If you can, think of one small thing that no one in your usual world would know and keep it secret. There's the true confirmation that the person is connected to the spirit world. I'm waiting for someone to tell me what's buried in my mother's coffin. No one has yet but they will and when they do, I'll know for sure the message is from my mother.

SNU – Spiritualists' National Union:

The Arthur Findlay College in Stansted, Essex, is the centre, the heart of the British Spiritualist movement. The college is responsible for spiritualist churches across the country, through Districts which deal with the churches on a week to week basis. The college has courses and offers certificates for speakers and demonstrators who prove to the college staff they are in fact connecting with spirit, not making it up as they go along.

Trance communications:

Some mediums go into trance when in circle, as the energy levels are very high and it seems a natural thing to do, to slide into a deep trance. The circle sitters provide the protection the medium needs whilst they are gone from this side of life. It is then the guides can come through and, using the medium's voice box, talk to the sitters.

Transfiguration:

This is when the medium's face changes, or is overlaid by the face of someone else for a very short time. It's another event that takes place in circle, when the energy levels are right and the sitters are there for protection.

A few more definitions to make things clearer for you

Aliens:

Do they visit us? Can we talk to them? If you ever doubt aliens have visited us, check out the Mayan and Aztec gods. They are totally surreal. Ask yourself where the Egyptian gods came from, bird heads, dog heads, what is the Sphinx… yes, aliens have visited us for countless thousands of years. Many are represented in ancient cultures in many ways. Consider the huge heads on Easter Island… the earth's indigenous people know of these 'visitors from other worlds' as my Cro-Magnon narrator refers to them. There are enough drawings in caves and carvings left by our ancestors to tell us this is so. All we need is an open mind to welcome them when they come.

There is a theory that some of us are Starseed; that we came from the planets and stars to colonise this earth, that we brought the spirits to the people. Check out Starseed on Google, see what you think. Does it fit well with you?

As it happens, I do have an alien guide. When he came, he showed himself as a large blue sphere. It took me a few minutes to realise why: The Martian Chronicles by Ray Bradbury is one of my all-time favourite books. Mr Bradbury depicts the Martians as floating blue spheres…

Angels:

Angels, as different from our 'walking alongside' guardian angels, that is. Angels are there to work with us, to answer such prayers as they can. Not all prayers can be answered for not all things can or should be given to us. They not always part of our pathway, so pleading for the One Love may get you nothing because he may not be that One Love, there may be someone else waiting to come into your life who will be better for you. That's pretty much how it works. They will answer what they can when they can and meantime make delightful companions.

Animal Totems:

We have animal spirits walking with us. It isn't necessarily your favourite animal, so your totem may surprise you, when you find out what it is. Mine is a red fox. How will you find out? As with so many things already mentioned, information will come via a message from a medium or a guide when you sit circle, or in your meditation you will find yourself walking with the same animal from time to time. A memory surfaced here of one circle sitter complaining she had a lion with her every time she meditated. This is spirit humour. This person declared she didn't like animals, so they gave her an animal totem that was big, fierce and could not be ignored...

Apports:

Apports are items which appear from nowhere – or so it seems. The truth is, they have been taken from somewhere and brought to you, if you're fortunate enough to be given something. So, the question is, have you at any time looked at something and said, 'I've never seen this before in my life'? A piece of jewellery, a dish, a bowl or, in the case of my friend Felicity Medland, a knife, a wooden spoon, items she knew she didn't own. They just arrived. Apports are when a spirit takes something from one place and puts it in another. It takes energy, so if it is done it is always done for a very good reason.

Djinns (or geniis, if you prefer):

Do these beings exist? They most definitely do. There are many different universes, each catering for its own particular being. Djinns are smoke elementals. Remember the genii coming from Aladdin's lamp? Depicting him as a puff of smoke that forms into a person is the only way the early storytellers could show a smoke elemental.

Long before this book was conceived as a project, I was studying the utterly stupid advertisements on eBay for rings, brooches, pendants, anything that was said to have 'trapped' a genii or djinn and if you were the person to release them, you could ask them to do anything. I found the advertisements highly amusing and was disappointed when eBay decided to ban that kind of paranormal paraphernalia from going on sale.

Djinns are selfish, they usually want to further their own aims and needs against yours but if you can appeal to their good nature – they do have one – they will do some things you ask. They crave human company and that's where you can get one over them, offer them companionship and then set them tasks for you. Another warning: be sensible. Don't ask them to give you lottery numbers, find the man of your dreams (or woman) the house of your dreams or anything that's beyond what you would normally do. They're not wizards, they're facilitators, if you like, so it has to stay within the bounds of logic and probability. That applies to everything you ask of spirit. It's a 'if it can be done, it will be done' syndrome. Like my getting the wages a week early – they were obviously already prepared, or she wouldn't have been able to hand them to me immediately. Spirit just chased things up a little.

Fairies:

Vexed question, do they exist? This seems a good point to mention an in-depth meditation I had some time ago and have not forgotten. I was walking through a wood and saw a tree with a door set in it. I opened the door which took me into the next realm, the Fairy Realm. They were everywhere, tiny, exquisite creatures fluttering around me, telling me to 'move on.' Another door awaited, I opened it and found myself in a world of dragons. None looked dangerous, but they were definitely watching me very closely, so I hurried to the next door, which opened into another wood where unicorns, centaurs and other horse-like creatures lived. Another door took me into a water world where mermaids, mermen, water nymphs and other sea going creatures lived.

All these realms coexist with ours side by side. Fairies, dragons, unicorns, they all exist – in their own realms. It's the visits others have made that has allowed us to know of their existence and the visits they occasionally make to this world give us the certainty of their existence.

Guardian Angels:

Guardian angels are something of a cliché for most people, but they really do exist. They may not all come with white robes and fantastic wings, but they are real, for all that.

There are beings in the Realms who devote themselves to serving us on this side of life. When you are born, a spirit/angel comes to be with you and, no matter what you do, think or say, they stay with you until you return home again. Their task is to guard you – hence guardian – and ensure you live the life span allocated to you, the one you agreed to before you came here.

The saying during the war was 'the bullet with your name on' will get you. It happens throughout life, if you think about it. How many times have you heard of people who missed a train/plane/ship, and something happened to it? If you really think of the 'miraculous' escapes some people have, a plane crash and people survive, or a train crash, who walks free from the wreckage or the biggest disaster of all, 9/11, how many people were not in the

Towers at that moment, for whatever reason? Delayed, at meetings, stopped from going in? It happens, and you will know many people who have been 'saved' or walked uninjured from, say, a car crash. That person was protected because it was not their time to go.

Your guardian angel is there to take good care of you. If you want a closer relationship with your angel, then sit quietly, light a candle and ask them to come close to you. Ask for a name and you will receive one. Then you can at least say thank you to the right angel who has taken such good care of you all this time.

Hauntings:

Are places haunted by ghosts? For me there is no such thing as a ghost and quite a few people agree with that. A ghost seems to be a snapshot of an action which is trapped in time. That is why the scenario, walking through a wall, for example, is repeated. A spirit would know the door is no longer there and not try and walk through it.

There is a 'mystery shopper' or should that be 'mystery employee' who walks through the shop. I have seen her twice. She dates from the early 60s judging by the hairstyle and clothes. She comes in the door and walks straight through, out the back. 'Out the back' in this time is a flat, when the property was completely renovated upstairs and down. I didn't know any different, was just left wondering where she went, until a very elderly lady came in and said 'oh, I see they blocked the door up.' I asked, 'what door?' and she said, 'the one out back to the store room.' So that's where my mystery lady goes, no doubt to leave her bag and coat and get ready to start work. She doesn't see any other spirits; those who walk with me say she doesn't acknowledge them. It's like the gentlemen's club meeting in my home.

So, haunted by ghosts? Very unlikely. If you visit and spirits are aware you're mediumistic, they will try and talk to you and let you know they're there, either guarding the property or choosing to remain there to see who they can talk to. One guide said, during a trance demonstration, some people choose to remain, to become 'advertisements' for the spirit world. That makes sense to me.

So there you are... ready to go... if you've not already got busy with meditation, questions and notebooks...

From here on out it's spirit all the way. I have just today been talking with someone who said a mutual friend has 'retired' from spiritual work. Nonsense, no such thing. Spirit don't let you go. Most of us don't want to be let go! Our roles change, the person I talked to had stopped doing clairvoyance but had become comforter and helper to people with life threatening conditions, being their shoulder to cry on, their driver to get them to hospital, just 'being there' for them. An essential role, if ever there was one.

Let me slide a comment in here, as I have done throughout this book... this lady is often in the café where I eat every Saturday, usually with friends. Today she was on her own; the friend she was waiting for hadn't turned up, another person she is helping. It gave us the chance to talk for the first time in ages. Meant to be? I was able to confirm to her she is a comforter, an essential role, and she confirmed to me, by the absence of her friend, that everything has its reason for happening, we needed to talk.

Spirit have their finger on your heart and mind, otherwise you wouldn't be reading this book. There are many other books out there to add to your ongoing library, books about Harry Edwards, England's greatest spiritual healer, the lovely little book Hiring the Heavens by Jean Slatter, which gave me such a boost when I needed it, an online book called Ask The Universe by Michael Samuels, another straightforward telling-it-like-it-is book on working with the energy of the Universe, and so many others. You will be directed to them without you realising it, and your library will grow with books spirit particularly want you to read. It's back to TRUST again.

Trust spirit to guide you, to walk with you, to comfort you and give you strength when you need it. They know we're all weak humans, we don't have their super-hyped energy to get us through; we need theirs. It will be given when you need it.

I've said this many times from the platform, in meetings, in readings, I'll say it again for you.

Once you accept spirit, your life will never be the same again. It will be rich beyond imagining with unconditional love, friendship and help.

What's stopping you? Get started!

When we meet up in the Realms when our earth lives are done, you can tell me how good it's been. Right?????

Michael Bentine shares his thoughts on reincarnation

Imagine, if you will, a chain link fence. It begins with a piece of carefully formed wire going up and up, linking itself around other equally carefully formed pieces of wire which in turn are linked around more pieces of wire. Each curve makes a diamond shape. Each twist of wire makes a connection.

You can view this chain link fence in many ways. It is a series of diamonds going up. It is a series of diamonds going sideways. It is a series of diamonds going diagonally. It is a series of diamonds going down. It is a set of wires linking with other wires. It has a start and it has a finish.

It is a barrier and it is a fence full of holes through which grasses, plants, small birds, small mammals and air can pass but humans cannot, not without cutting it. Sometimes litter blows against it and is trapped. Larger birds sit on top of it and survey the world.

Here and there along its course it has supports, thick posts which hold it. The wire is stapled or nailed to that support.

Sometimes the wire rusts and becomes weak. Sometimes it is bright and strong and holds up against the world.

Sometimes it is taken down, rolled up and thrown away. Sometimes it is replaced with new bright shiny wire fencing.

Sometimes it is taken down and nothing is put in its place, the air, the plants, the birds, mammals, litter and people are free to walk through into the place it once guarded.

Sometimes it is taken down and a new, different fence is put up, or a wall of brick or stone, designed to keep people and animals out.

There are always changes in our lives; there is nothing so permanent as change. But the chain link fence concept is the best one right now to describe the way past lives work. We will revert to the other analogies throughout the book but let us stay with the fence for the moment.

The chain link fence is your/our/everyone's past, present and future lives. Every horizontal line of diamonds is a period of history. Every vertical and diagonal line of diamonds is a life. Each life is entwined with countless others as it goes up and as it goes down.

The chain link fence encompasses the entire known and unknown Universe. It curves at the top and at the bottom to make a complete ball. In truth there is no beginning and there is no end. There are countless billions of souls. Those who have completed their course of past life lessons are inside. Those who are still learning are inside.

Please note this carefully: *no one is outside*.

And they never will be.

***

Where are you in the chain link fence at this time? About half way up the diamonds? If so, you have a good many past lives behind you already. You may have experienced that sense of déjà vu when you went somewhere or met someone, that instant of 'knowing' you have been there before or met them before this! If you have, that is the jumping off point to find out who you were in whatever time span of history that happened to be.

There are some who say that past lives are not of any interest to us today, but I beg to differ. Past lives can resolve some of the phobias or traumas we suffer in this life. Each life we have lived was carefully considered and discussed before we came here. Each brought us new experiences, new conflicts, new traumas and new occasions for pure happiness. Each was for a reason. Therefore it makes sense, surely, to accept that the information we gather through each life is imbedded in our soul and accordingly, it must of necessity reveal itself from time to time. When we arrive on earth to start our new life, pushed out into the world to make our way as best we can for as long as we chose to, practically all the knowledge we have acquired, slowly and painfully, over hundreds of years, is wiped out of our conscious minds. It is only later, as we develop and our soul grows with us, do we get hints and snippets of what we already know.

That doesn't go for everyone, though. Think at this moment of the midwife who looks at a new-born child and says, 'this one has been here before' for the knowledge is there, in the eyes which should be blank and new and ready to absorb but are not, they are full of wisdom already. The child will not know it immediately but soon enough the information will filter through. There is no way of doing research on this, but it seems reasonable to speculate, with a degree of certainty, that those who arrive with a considerable amount of pre-knowledge are the ones who become the loners, the thinkers, the writers, the artists, the composers, the leaders, for they stand out from the crowd from birth and continue to stand out throughout their lives. Ask yourself if you know such people or are one yourself. It could also be speculated, with a degree of certainty, that you are one of these people, which is why you were drawn to this part of the book. It's confirming what you already know and giving you nothing new. Confirmation, though, is always good and if this fills in a few blanks along the way, pieces that you needed to complete your own soul picture, then it's worthwhile.

***

Before a chain link fence can be manufactured, it has to be planned, how many 'diamonds' high will it be, 3 ft, 4 ft, and so on.

We are souls. We are individual souls making a journey that can last for eternity, if we so desire. We begin beyond this earth, we begin in the Realms where souls live and are prepared for their progression. All souls need to progress. There are lessons to be learned, concepts to be discovered and experiences to be lived through. Nothing is random, nothing is 'by chance'; there is no such thing as coincidence. Each time a soul is about to come back to earth, there is a pre-planning session at which we meet our prospective parents, partners, lifelong friends, whoever it takes to give us the particular life experiences we need. As we progress, as we go through life after life, we meet these same people over and over again but in different roles. In one life they may be our parents, our marriage partner or our friends. In another they may be our siblings, our offspring, our enemies, but always there is a connection. It is these people you meet in this life when you know, without a word being spoken, that there is a bond between you that cannot be identified immediately. Sometimes you never do identify it, you just accept. It is a past life bond that cannot be broken.

It is very difficult for some people to accept that the broken, difficult, traumatic and sometimes curtailed lives they lead were planned by them before they came, but it is a fact. It is the only thing, the only concept, which makes sense of what would otherwise appear to be random accidents, incidents, broken relationships, intense happiness and equally intense unhappiness, bitterness and loneliness. It is all part of the learning experience you chose before you came. Because of that, you know that whatever happens, you will have the strength to survive it.

Finally...

Time to leave this book and go channel some words. There are more people channelling than ever, but the demand is greater than the people available can cope with. I have had to turn down many wonderful names I would dearly love to have worked with, but there aren't enough years for me to do it all. If you are called to channel, go with it. The words, the work, will enchant you from the beginning, the ease with which it all comes will be a surprise and a joy and the satisfaction is immense.

If I've encouraged you to become a medium and you begin bringing comfort and solace to the bereaved, my job is well done. Walk tall and proud for you are one of the chosen, the ones spirit have marked as their own. There are a lot of us and yet there aren't enough of us, the world needs healers, peacemakers, comforters, psychics to bring good news – and bad if necessary and you will know the difference when it happens – and generally they need more servants, workers, believers...

Whatever sacrifice you make for them will be worth it: they will respond and give you a whole new life in return. I have not regretted a single moment of my life with spirit. With their blessing, yours will be the same.

My Books

In alphabetical order

All You Need To Know About Spirit – question and answer booklet.

Brief and Bitter Hearts – the life of Guy Fawkes

Captain of the Wight with Edward Woodville

Cast In Stone – Mayan Divination - Redwood

Daniel – A Life – the life and death of the sad clown Daniel

Death Be Pardoner To Me – the life of George, duke of Clarence

Fools and Kings and Fighting Men – the life of Charles I

I Diced With God – the life of Henry VIII

Living In The Shadow Of The Cross – Archangel Gabriel

Not The Shadow Of A Man – the life of Jacquetta Woodville

The Darker Side of Henry VIII – Henry's six Queens give their side of the story

Thirty Pieces of Silver – the last three years of the life of Judas Iskariot

Books or downloads are available from fiction4all.com

My Short Stories

If you want to read any of these spirit dictated stories, email me at Servantofspirit@gmail.com and I'll send you a copy – free!

The Fragrance of a Poisoned Flower – George Villiers, duke of Buckingham
The Hunger of the Moon – Virgil 'Gus' Grissom
Countdown to Death – Antony Woodville
Towton Nightmare – Antony Woodville
Blood on the Rose – Kathryn Howard
The Day Death Wore Boots – Yul Brynner
Transformation – Bela Lugosi
I Bid You Welcome by Bela Lugosi
The Pied Piper's Story by Roald Dahl
The Kingmaker is Dead, Long Live the King – Richard Neville, Earl of Warwick

Acknowledgements

Sending thanks to those special people who contributed and continue to contribute to my journey with spirit – in alphabetical order:

Penny Barton (aka Pagan) who sent tarot readings to me via her website

Hazel Butterworth (no longer with us) who shared Daniel with me and so much more

Ann Davies for spirit portraits, readings, advice, friendship

Stuart Holland for simply being there when needed – always, and for publishing the books and help and multiple connections on the spiritual level

Mary Holliday for being the best, best friend anyone ever had.

Ken L Jones in California, someone on my spiritual wavelength who sends a poem every day for me to think on.

Derek Marney (no longer with us) for advice and friendship

Felicity Medland, daughter of the great healer **Harry Edwards**, for friendship, memories together with gifts of exquisite needlepoint portraits of Henry's queens and serene landscape oil paintings.

Alan J Miles, medium and Brian Jones fan, who was good enough to channel the poem for me. Later he wrote a book on Brian which my company published for him.

David Millard (no longer with us) for friendship and laughter.

Brian and Shirley Rice for years of circle and even more years of friendship

Charles Samway (no longer with us) for the messages

Edward Sayers (no longer with us) for being there for me and for Derek.

Eugene Stewart for Druidic thoughts, support, friendship and love

Terry Wakelin (no longer with us) who supported me long before he believed

Norman Wilson for endless energy and friendship

***

I wish to mention here those guides and companions who have walked with me and those who continue to walk with me, each for their own reasons and each with their special skills to help me work:

Henry VIII, who would not be anywhere else but first… we shared so much and still do.

Dave Allen, who helps me write humorous advertising copy which has attracted a following and benefited the shop.

Michael Bentine who is a regular visitor and whose book The Door Into Summer was very meaningful during my development.

William Blake, who brings me poetry and commendations on the work I do in the shop – and who works with Ken Jones in California to help him

158

get his poems to the wider world. It's connections, always the connections.

Sir Winston Churchill who calls himself 'your big man', ever there for strength I can lean on. I have too, many times.

Jesus Christ – what more can I say?

Ezekiel, one of my Biblical guides and helpers, with his own tasks with me and in the spirit world.

Archangel Gabriel, my guardian angel and companion.

Joshua and Judas, two more of my Biblical guides and helpers, with their own tasks with me and in the spirit world.

Brian Jones, who walks with me for companionship and to bring me music.

Kicking Bear, Sitting Bull's nephew, who brings me strength and wisdom.

Cardinal Thomas Lindenwood, for religious and spiritual advice.

Mickey, Leslie Flint's Cockney guide, providing laughter always and philosophy sometimes. I have had very accurate messages whilst sitting circle.

Moses, another Biblical guide and helper, who has his own tasks in the spirit world and still finds time for me.

Redwood, my incredible Mayan guide.

Sitting Bull, in charge of the spiritual progress of those around me.

Snow who, among other things, went on a deeply spiritual pilgrimage for me.

Dr Horst Sturtgarten, a past life husband who comes the moment I am ill to give advice and dispense spirit potions. The rest of the time he teaches others who want to learn of herbs and potions to assist in healing work.

Antony Woodville, a past life husband who is rarely far from my side, bringing humour, help and overwhelming love, the person I consider my true soul mate. If this book has been easy to read, it's down to Antony. He was the author of the first book printed in England by William Caxton.

Jacquetta Woodville who helps when I read my tarot cards.

Lightning Source UK Ltd.
Milton Keynes UK
UKHW022044170820
368379UK00006B/436